CRAVEN'S WAR
A MATTER OF HONOUR

NICK S. THOMAS

Copyright © 2022 Nick S. Thomas

All rights reserved.

ISBN: 979-8327116375

PROLOGUE

The armies of France were driven from Portugal for the third time, but every advance into Spain has come at a huge cost. Increasing numbers of French troops had forced Wellington to retreat into Portugal once more, but this time it was different. The allied army did not have to run to the protection of the Royal Navy nor the lines of Torres Vedras, they had held firm at the border with Spain. A standoff at the border which neither side risked crossing, for it would be such a huge gamble that one defeat could change the course of the war in a single day. The frustrating stalemate, however, was a significant improvement.

But stagnation and stability bring with it new troubles for Wellington's army as they turn to stealing, drinking, gambling, and duelling to pass the time and take out their frustrations on one another. None are more familiar with this than Captain Craven who faces a fine balancing act, as he struggles to maintain discipline and keep Timmerman and Hawkshaw from tearing one another apart. Many grand battles lay ahead, but now the officers of Wellington's army must maintain order so that the army is ready to fight when the time comes.

CHAPTER 1

"Make ready! Present!" Craven roared.

His orders needed no translation, for the Portuguese troops had become extremely familiar with the orders of command for musketry, even if they spoke little to no English otherwise. A full company of Portuguese line infantry readied their muskets, formed into two lines, replicating the thin red line in all but colour. They moved with the same discipline and skill as their red-coated counterparts as they took aim at another line of infantry. They were similarly equipped but had been stripped to their shirts, making the bodies of soldiers' contrast distinct.

"Fire!" Craven cried.

Flints hit steel as the frizzens were launched forward and sparks flew, but not a single flash in the pan for any man as a chorus of flintlocks being dry fried echoed out across the dry and still plain. The same orders were cried out by Ferreira commanding those who opposed them, in what appeared to be the smallest of pitched battles. Two companies engaged as if they were meeting one another at Talavera, what felt like a lifetime ago and yet still remained fresh in many memories.

"Prepare to charge!"

The Portuguese Company brought their muskets to the port position.

"Charge!"

They began their advance as those opposing them in their white shirts did the same, yet there was no cold steel glistening in the sun. For the bayonet affixed to every man's musket wore its sheath and was well tied onto the muzzle of each weapon so as to create a safe training device.

"Charge bayonets!"

Craven rode beside the infantry, spurring them on with his sword drawn, the only bare blade in sight. All officers had been given a singlestick in place of their swords. The front rank brought their bayonets down almost parallel to the ground before a war cry echoed out, and the two sides charged into one another with much enthusiasm and ferocity. They knocked aside bayonets and thrust their own home. They did not hold back much compared to fighting the French, ramming home their blunted bayonets with enough force to crack ribs if they landed. Each man who was struck by a thrust went down to one knee, whilst many threw in almost full power strikes with the butts of their muskets to subdue their opponents and create openings. The two fiercely competitive companies battled it out, neither willing to submit to the other. Yet without the threat of death, neither would break and run as so often happened during a bayonet charge. They battled it out to the last man standing, which was a most unusual affair. And yet it was a vivid reminder of the savage bayonet contest at Sabugal, where the British and French infantry had bitterly fought for an hour over a single howitzer, neither willing to concede, no matter the cost.

Craven and Ferreira watched the chaos ensue as blood was drawn from several blows to the jaws and noses of those fighting, although there were no complaints. The men on either side wanted victory above all else, fighting so fiercely as if they imagined they were indeed fighting the French. It was a close affair by the two bodies of troops who had received all the same training. Finally, they were whittled down to a single man on either side in the most balanced contest one could ever see. Those who were knelt downplaying dead cried out in support of their man as they circled one another. The brave fighters thrust and parried, swinging in strikes against one another. Parry after parry was made until they were locked together like two bulls, their muskets braced between them. One man reached out and punched the other in the jaw, causing him to stagger back and break the stalemate. A cheer rang out, but it was not a scoring blow to end the contest.

"Come on!" Craven shouted. He was on the side of the bloody nosed man.

The bloody soldier thrust back at his attacker, but with one quick beat his musket was thrown from his hands, and he was driven down onto his back. A celebratory cry rang out from the opposing side, those under the command of Ferreira.

"Finish it!" Ferreira roared excitedly for having got one over Craven.

His man towered over the other and retracted his musket and bayonet, as if to ram it home with enough force to kill even with the covered bayonet. But the one on his back pushed off from the ground with his feet and smashed his shoe into the groin of the man towering over him. A collective cry of pain rang out from the troops of both sides as if every soldier there felt the painful impact in their most tender area. The excruciating pain was enough to cause an instant reaction, releasing the man's hold of his weapon and cupping his groin. He collapsed face first into the dirt as his body gave way from under him. His attacker leapt to his feet and scooped up the musket and bayonet as the wounded man clambered back to his feet, only to find the bayonet pressed against his chest. A wild cheer roared from those under Craven's command at having snatched victory from the jaws of defeat.

"Lopo! Lopo! Lopo!" the men cried out the name of the victor who danced around triumphantly.

"We win," smiled Craven.

"The hell you did! Your man cheated!" Ferreira protested in anger.

"I don't see it that way, and I don't think there is a man here who does," snapped Craven.

But there were already grumblings amongst the men under Ferreira's command, which spurred him on to protest further.

"A friendly contest you said, with only the point of the bayonet scoring a hit."

"Yes? And?"

"A kick in the private parts is no scoring hit."

"No, but the bayonet thrust which followed it was," replied Craven to a cheer of those on his side.

"My side could have played as dirty a game, but they did not for respect for their fellow soldiers," snarled Ferreira.

It was an unusually passionate plea from the Portuguese

officer who rarely cared so much so long as he was alive and not having to do too much work. Yet now he was as passionate as the most competitive man in the army, revealing the change in heart he had experienced as the war had progressed.

"Come on, Ferreira, no man fought a clean fight here. They did what they had to do to win. You're just angry that my man showed greater initiative. He found a way to win, just like we do every time we go into battle."

"Then replay the game, so that we may get an accurate result under fairer conditions," demanded Ferreira.

Groans rang out from those who understood what he was asking for. Craven sighed as he didn't much have a care for floundering under the afternoon sun for any longer.

"It seems you find yourselves quite stuck!" Hunt roared as he rode into the scene with Paget whilst Matthys, Charlie, and Caffy watched from a small embankment, laying about with nothing to do but enjoy the show.

"It seems we have a winner!" Charlie shouted in celebration of Craven's success.

"He did not win anything!" Ferreira scowled.

Paget looked confused.

"It seems Mr Ferreira believes a fight must be won fairly," smiled Craven.

"Is that how you fight the French?" Paget asked.

Ferreira looked even more furious now, but before anything could erupt, it was Hunt who proposed a solution, smiling all the way, and leaving the others hanging on eagerly for the solution he was to propose.

"You see the contest as over, but I see two men still on the field, one on either side," he grinned. Paget looked confused, but Craven and Ferreira knew precisely to what he was referring to.

"You would have us fight?" Ferreira asked astonishment.

"These two fine companies put on a tremendous and most pleasing display. They fought hard and they fought well, but their company commanders are yet to join the fray. They merely watched on as they poured sweat and blood upon the land. I say they join the men they commanded and decide this contest not with words, but actions!"

The Portuguese troops roared with excitement, as they did not even need to understand his words to know precisely what he was calling for. It was an exciting prospect for all watching. Ferreira did not look impressed, but he knew he could not back down with any dignity left. He jumped down from his horse and dropped his sword belt to the ground, taking a singlestick from one of the officers who had battled it out on the field before them. Craven smiled as he did the same, relishing every second of it. They both knew it was a far from fair manner to settle the dispute, for Craven was one of the finest swordsmen in the army. Yet Ferreira did not protest and had himself became quite the accomplished fencer, particularly in the days the two men had spent with De Rosas and Vicenta.

"This should be good," smiled Hunt mischievously.

Paget could tell Archie was toying with the two Captains, but he did not mind it. It was all a little harmless fun and a good morale booster if nothing else for the Portuguese troops who once again found themselves having to defend their border from the French. The two Captains got into guard as they faced off with one another. The sweat-soaked Portuguese troops watched on, glad of the rest as much as the entertainment.

"First to three strikes shall we call it?" Archie demanded, as he played to the crowd and prolonged the contest as long as possible.

The two swordsmen began to circle one another in perfect sequence as if they were dancing and each looked for an opening. Craven carried a huge smile on his face as if he were enjoying every moment, but in his confidence, he had lost some focus, and Ferreira suddenly lashed out. Craven reacted at the last moment, but Ferreira's blade looped around his guard, seemingly striking on the other side. As Craven responded, Ferreira turned it again and struck from underneath, lashing the stick into Craven's elbow. It was a stinging blow, as much for the solid ash striking bone as it was to Craven's pride. Not only had he been struck, but he had not landed the first blow. A cheer rang out, but he took it in his stride and smiled in response, confidently concealing his frustration behind the knowledge he could easily strip away Ferreira's early lead.

Both Captains probed for a weakness as they played at long distance, launching the smallest of feints and half cuts and thrusts, provoking the responses they wanted and looking for any sign of weakness and any opening which could be exploited. The interaction was so precise, and in such harmony, as could ever be seen by two fighters not only experts of their craft, but also intimately familiar with one another.

Craven lowered his singlestick off to one side, giving a huge invitation. Ferreira took it, but knowing it was a trap, launched a feint into it. Craven had planned for that and timed a perfect counter. He turned his wrist and snapped a quick ascending cut into Ferreira's wrist with enough force to make it go numb for a moment. Ferreira had gotten overconfident and forgotten who he was fighting, thinking he could play a middling trick and get away with it. It was one all as they both came back to guard. The audience watched silently, enthralled by the display of skill and forgetting for a moment the reason it was even being fought.

Ferreira smiled before launching forward. He cut high to Craven's inside and then to his outside before swinging down for the leg. Craven slipped his leg back safely but had no time to counter as Ferreira pressed forward with continuous rotational ascending blows; the blade wheeling in front of his face as he laid on blow after blow, seeming like he would never stop until he landed one. Craven circled way to get space as he parried each blow. He finally tried to time a shot between the blows, but it had been just what Ferreira had been waiting for. He stopped mid-swing, and with a quick beat with the back of his stick, cast Craven's weapon aside for the briefest of moment to land the blow he had so desperately sought. Ferreira's singlestick lashed in and clipped Craven's chin, opening up a small cut, but also surprising and staggering him a little. For a moment Ferreira looked concerned he might have hurt his friend and fellow officer, but Craven soon recovered. The playfulness in his expression was gone and replaced with fury. Ferreira was one strike away from victory, and Craven suddenly realised how desperate the situation was. He went forward and engaged Ferreira's stick on his inside, continually walking forward, seemingly daring the Portuguese officer to strike around his stick. When it did not come, Craven swung for the right side of Ferreira's face with a heavy blow. Ferreira lifted up to parry it to find the stick had already re-directed and smashed into the side of his knee, causing him to wince in pain as his leg buckled a little.

"Come on, Craven!" Paget roared.

Craven was not playing anymore, but fighting to win, as if he were fighting to survive. Ferreira attacked but more cautiously this time, not taking any risks. Strike after strike and parry were made until finally, Ferreira saw a small opening to land a quick thrust. He extended forward, and yet his target was gone in a flash. Craven nimbly leapt to one side, avoiding the attack completely. He struck back with a brisk blow of his own to Ferreira's chin to repay him in kind. A roar rang out from the troops on both sides. The contest's purpose had been forgotten by many, and they merely celebrated a fine end to a hard-fought battle between highly skilled swordsmen. Ferreira patted Craven on the back in appreciation for a good contest, but it was clear Craven was still stuck in the mindset of a fight. He flinched a little at the contact as if needing to make a riposte, but as he looked into Ferreira's friendly eyes, he calmed himself and returned to normality.

"You fought well," he admitted.

"I will admit I am more than a little proud that I was not a walk over," smiled Ferreira.

"Far from it, you were a most formidable opponent."

"Come on, Craven, we both know you were not giving it your all," smirked Ferreira.

But Craven shrugged as it sure felt like he had. Matthys approached, smiling broadly having enjoyed the display and glad to see that bloody war had been replaced by friendly contest with all in good spirits.

"The men are in fine spirits!"

Craven nodded in agreement. After the bleak funeral, and

foul and bitter business which had transpired between Hawkshaw and Timmerman, it was a welcome relief and return to normality. His brother had watched from afar, still resting from his wounds suffered at Timmerman's hands.

"We should be on our way back to Lisbon, for our time there was cut well short," insisted the Sergeant.

Craven nodded along passively as he seemed to duck the idea.

"They did well, did they not? Both companies fought hard and well," he replied.

"As well as any redcoat I should say. They fight like men who protect their homeland and have been given the training and knowhow to do so with the utmost skill," replied Matthys.

"Yes, well they will be needing it," added Ferreira.

"You fear another invasion? You believe the French would invade for a fourth time?" Matthys asked.

"Why would they not? Wellington was not strong enough to march across Spain, and now the wolves are at the gate once more. Either they come for us, or we go after them. Those are the only two options."

"This standoff cannot last forever. Eventually, one side must cross over," added Craven.

"But we need not be there at the forefront when whichever way it goes," replied Matthys in a pained tone.

Craven grimaced, knowing more complaints were about to follow, and he could not get a word in before Matthys launched into them.

"You promised we would step away from all of this, at least for a while. God knows we all need it. Perhaps you more than any of us."

"Did we not take our time in Lisbon?"

"We tried, but we were met by more violence and more tragedy. We came out here to see Colonel Bevan laid to rest with honour, and yet a week later we are still here because you volunteered us for more duties."

"Duty? Is that not what we are here for?"

"You have done more than enough, we all have. The Salfords have been pushed beyond breaking point, and you cannot ask them to keep on going as they have been."

"I am not sure the French share your opinion, for they keep on coming."

"Damn it, James, why do you have to be so damned stubborn?"

He said it quietly so as to not share their dispute with all the soldiers around them. Though Matthys went on relentlessly despite his quiet low volume.

"There are many more men to fight this war. We must step away from it, at least for a while or it will consume us all. We will all follow you to hell and back, we have shown that many times, but every man has a breaking point," he insisted, revealing and openly admitting his own fragility without any shame.

Craven took a long and pained breath as he mulled it over, but he would not commit to anything, as he looked back to the two companies of Portuguese infantrymen they had been given command over to enrich their training. They were in good spirits and chatted freely, reliving and re-enacting some of the actions of the fight which had been such a close-run thing. All ill will had fallen away, despite the many cuts and bruises, and they went on as brothers. Matthys wanted to press on and say more, but their attention was drawn by the sound of musket fire, sporadic and not within sight, but it could not be too far away. Two horsemen burst out from the words ahead of them, both wearing Portuguese uniforms and galloping as fast as they could, fleeing from the direction of the gunfire. Several more shots rang out, but the scene fell silent once more. The two Portuguese companies looked in amazement as the two riders approached at speed.

"Gather your cartridge boxes! Form up!" Craven pulled on his uniform and sword belt.

The subalterns quickly took over, roaring the same commands in Portuguese as the men rushed to the piles of tunics, cartridge boxes, and shakos.

"Have them loaded and ready to fight," Craven ordered Ferreira as he took out his spyglass for a better look.

"What is it, Sir?" Paget asked.

"It is trouble we do not need. We are not here to fight," insisted Matthys.

"You would leave them to do it alone?" snapped Craven as he looked as the Portuguese troops who had only young and experienced subalterns to lead them, the body of troops having been left in Craven's hands as they conducted training. Matthys didn't like it, but he could not protest, not wanting to see them left to the mercy of whatever approached either.

The Portuguese troops hurried to load their muskets, and the clang of ramrods sliding down their muzzles echoed out, but through the ground they could feel the thundering hooves of the approaching riders who moved with incredible urgency. Through his spy glass, Craven could see the look of fear on the faces of the two men who looked desperate to relay a message but unable to do so until they reached the newly formed up lines.

Craven leapt onto his horse and cocked both locks of his double-barrelled pistol and slightly adjusted all of his equipment, readying everything for a fight at a moment's notice.

"We aren't prepared to do battle," insisted Matthys who formed up beside him.

Only Craven and Ferreira were mounted, for the rest of the horses of the Salfords' had been tied up over the far ridge and out of the way of their exercises.

"Should I gather our horses, Sir?" Paget asked. He was eager to retrieve Augustus for both his sake and his cherished horses also.

"No!" Craven snapped without giving any explanation.

He did not want to risk any of them travelling across open ground and away from the protection of the infantry forces he now had at his command. Two hundred troops were under his command, but they were not riflemen nor the battle-hardened troops Gamboa had led to join the Salfords. They were mostly inexperienced, but eager and well trained. They were now silent as they waited with their muskets shouldered. Their bayonets glistened in the afternoon sun, finally having had their sheaths untied and removed so as to take them from a safe training tool to deadly cold steel. Ferreira rushed to Craven's side as the two horsemen closed the final yards and came to an abrupt halt.

"We are under attack by French cavalry!" one man roared, having a good grasp of English and addressing Craven with it, seeing his officer's red jacket.

"How many?"

"Hard to say, but we were twenty-five and were swept aside like we were nothing. It could be one hundred, two hundred, maybe more!"

He cried out so loudly that many of the Portuguese troops who had a grasp of the language heard, and whispers soon spread the information across the lines. Craven grimaced at the sight, knowing their morale had just taken a beating before any fight had even started.

"No army has crossed over. It must be a raiding party," insisted Ferreira.

"They are testing us," replied Craven.

"We should withdraw to the protection of our lines," Matthys added.

"Our pickets are almost a mile away and cavalry bear down upon us. No, I would not have them show their backs," said Craven as he looked to the poor Portuguese infantrymen with visions of French sabres hacking at their backs.

"We are not ready for a fight," insisted Matthys.

But Craven ignored him as he rode along in front of the two companies.

"Frenchmen approach. They approach Portuguese soldiers on Portuguese ground, would you give it to them, or will you stand and fight?"

A cheer rang out as they thrust their bayonetted muskets high into the air, the collective roar lifting their spirits from what the messenger had lost.

"Prepare for battle!"

Craven rode back to the few Salfords he had by his side and the two Portuguese cavalrymen who had delivered the message.

"You mean to stand against them?" the messenger asked in amazement.

"If we all ran in the face of the French, then this war would have been over years ago. I would not have our efforts wasted, would you?"

The man looked a little ashamed, but it was not Craven's intent.

"Will you fight with us?"

The man looked back up with pride.

"We will."

"Then let's give those bastards hell!"

CHAPTER 2

They could hear the thunder of hooves, and a dust cloud rose up from behind the treeline ahead of them. A great force was bearing down on them, and there was nothing they could do now but stand and weather it.

"Should we form square, Sir?" Paget asked.

"We don't have enough men," replied Ferreira.

Craven nodded in agreement.

"With too few we would be trampled over, a breach would quickly be found, and it would all be over. All we can do is resist them with all that we have, every musket and every inch of cold steel."

"And if it is not enough, Sir?"

"Then we will die here, but I would rather die facing forward than with a sabre in my back."

"How did they get through? How could so many cavalry get through our lines?" Paget pleaded.

"The same way they have throughout this whole war, because armies hold an area. A city or some municipality, but not an entire border," Ferreira said.

"Have we not done the same to them throughout?" Craven asked, as he remembered all the times they had ridden into enemy territory, striking targets that were thought far from danger.

Paget shrugged. He knew thew they were both right, but it didn't make it any easier to stomach. Especially as the last thing he had expected this day was the bloody barbarity of war. It was hot and the rancid smell of walnut trees had filled the air, a putrid smell so revolting that neither the nearby olive groves nor the gusts of wind passing through the valley could conceal it. And yet despite the foul odour, it was a far more welcome experience to the sulphur filled air of musket fire and the horrific sights, sounds, and stink of dead and dying soldiers which would follow. Paget had expected an easy day, an enjoyable one in fact. The sort which made soldiering seem more like one great big adventure, filled with sports and festivities. Never could he have imagined it would have been reduced to a bloody battle, so much so that he was not at all prepared for it, having left both his rifle and pistol on the saddle of Augustus, and he had only his sword for his own defence.

The restlessness was on all the faces of the Portuguese troops who waited for the storm to lash them. They had marched out this day in good spirits and put all efforts into what they expected to be a gruelling but not lethal day of training, a stark contrast to what they were now facing. Craven rode along their front lines once again. They were formed up in two ranks, just as was so commonly seen with British regulars, which was hardly surprising, as they had received a close mirror of the redcoats training. Officially, British troops were to form in three ranks, but they were rarely seen in more than two, except when making or receiving a charge. They might indeed receive a charge from whatever French forces approached, but Craven was relying on firepower more than anything else. The massed firepower of well training infantrymen. He knew it was a risky strategy, but if they could not deal significant damage to those advancing on them, then none of it would matter. What good would a stronger formation be if they could not hold, and nobody was coming to relieve them?

Solace came in one form, and that was the knowledge that the French cavalry could not be any more than a scouting and raiding party. They could not and would not advance so close to Anglo Portuguese lines with anything but a very small force, or an extremely large one, and this was most certainly the former, as a vast army could not move so quickly into Portuguese territory without forewarning.

It was a numbers game now as Craven calculated it in his head. Cavalry would close the distance quickly. The Portuguese lines might manage two volleys if they remembered their training and held firm. Four hundred musket balls, enough to make an impact, but it all depended on the French strength. He wondered how many Frenchmen they could down in those volleys, Forty? Fifty? If they were lucky. Would it be enough to dissuade a cavalry force? Would it be enough to make a difference if it came to a clash of cold steel? The prospect of cavalry crashing into a thin and unsupported line of infantry in open ground was a horrifying one. A situation to be avoided at all costs, for it frequently led to the complete destruction of the poor souls on foot, and yet that was the situation Craven was about to find himself in. The only two questions which remained were how many Frenchmen would burst out from the trees ahead, and whether the Portuguese would stand to resist them?

"Remember what you are fighting for! Remember all the battles your countrymen have fought! Remember all the sacrifices which have been made! Do not let them be for nothing!"

The Portuguese Subalterns repeated his words in their own language all down the line. A line little more than one hundred long and two deep. It was a tiny force, the smallest spec on the wide-open landscape. They could see the glimmer of movement through the woods and knew the time had come. Craven went back to the few Salfords he had come out to the border with. They had four rifles between them, and then just their swords. Hawkshaw looked as ready as any for a fight, but he was still recovering his wounds. Although, Craven knew they needed every fighter they could muster, even those at half strength, and so he said nothing to his brother. The French cavalry reached the treeline ahead. They moved at a gentle canter but seemed to perk up with excitement at the sight of the Portuguese infantry. A lonely thin dark blue line.

"Make ready!"

The orders soon echoed out as the French cavalry fanned out ahead of them, ready to make their advance. An excitable officer led from the front, waving his sword about his head as if looking upon the Portuguese troops as easy prey.

"Take him down," Craven ordered Ferreira.

The Caçadores Captain dismounted and gave his horse to Hawkshaw.

"Take him, for I will do better down here."

Hawkshaw did not need to be told twice, for the mount would more than make up for his weakened state. Ferreira took aim and fired, striking the officer in the chest and causing him to look in horror at the gaping hole in his chest before collapsing from his horse. A cry of celebration rang out from the Portuguese lines, just as Craven hoped it would. He had robbed the enemy of their commanding officer whilst simultaneously smashing the morale of the enemy and stealing it for his own forces, as they now held firm and looked ready for anything. Ferreira hurried to reload with a smug expression.

"Work your way through their officers and then their sergeants," whispered Craven to the few rifles he had beside him. It was not many, but more than enough to ruin the French command structure as he watched the next man take over and order an advance.

"Present!" Craven roared as the Portuguese infantry lowered their muskets until two hundred muskets with their bayonets all bristling forward were levelled at the French cavalry as they gained pace.

"Fire!"

A volley ripped out, and Craven saw many of the cavalrymen knocked from their horses before the whole line was shrouded in powder smoke. It was intoxicating, for the wind only came in gusts and the valley was now still.

"Load!"

The scrape of ramrods soon echoed out. Ferreira was reloaded before the line, and the powder smoke dissipated just enough that he could see the enemy. He knelt down and took aim as he picked his target. He spotted a grizzled-looking sergeant with a large moustache and mutton chops. He looked the sort which would rally men to his side and spur them on to fight. Ferreira fired and killed him outright. He hurried to reload, but the cavalry were now just fifty yards away, and he knew there was no chance of reloading. So, he took his rifle in his left hand, the butt stock facing forward, and drew out his sabre with his right.

"Present!" Craven ordered, desperately hoping to get one more volley in at point-blank range where it would also be most effective. For it was hard to miss, and the flames of the muzzles would scorch those ahead of them and strike fear into the charging horses.

"Fire!"

The cavalry were ten yards out when the volley was unleashed. Many of the Frenchmen were blasted from their saddles whilst some horses threw their riders regardless. The huge cloud of powder smoke encircled them all as if a great fog had descended. The French cavalrymen who did reach the line of infantry were disordered. They had lost much of their pace in the devastating salvo, yet some managed to plough into the Portuguese line at full tilt and crashed through.

"Hold!"

Craven could only see a couple of yards as the cavalrymen who had punched through the line vanished once more. He knew they must be dealt with but did not want to leave the line.

"Go!" Paget shouted to him.

Craven dug in his heels and spurred his horse on after one of the cavalrymen who had smashed though. He rushed out from the powder fog and could see the Frenchman had already wheeled around ready to charge into the rear of the infantry, and a second was coming around as well. In a battle one or two stragglers would be of little concern, but with such a small infantry force, he knew they could cause chaos. The two Frenchmen soon turned their attention to him, but Hawkshaw galloped up to his flank to even the odds, not caring for his weak body. But at their backs they could hear the clash of cold steel and the cries of soldiers being cut and stabbed. It was complete chaos, but for the cloud of powder smoke they could not tell which way the battle swayed. Craven did not want to waste any more time away from the fight. He drew out his pistol and took aim, shooting one out of the saddle before turning the second barrel on the other, and striking him down before he could react. Hawkshaw looked stunned.

"Come on!" Craven shouted as he turned back to the fight.

Hawkshaw was still stunned by the seemingly savage display. He had expected some kind of honourable affair as if he had arrived for a duel, but Craven had killed both men in an instance without any chance of a fair fight. There was no time to argue over it and no one to argue with, as Craven was already galloping back into the fog. He rushed on after his brother, into the intoxicating powder fog which clung to the once peaceful field which had erupted into a savage battle. It was more like a small corner of what one might see on a large-scale battle than one would expect of a small skirmish. The fog began to lift a little as Hawkshaw caught sight of Craven. He was in the midst of plunging his sword into a Frenchman's chest, and yet the man slumped off to one side before he could retrieve his prized sword. Ans so his victim fell with the sword still embedded in him. Craven then scooped up the Frenchman's sabre as it fell from the dying man's grasps and took it for his own.

Craven made the most of the broad and well curved heavy cutting blade. He swung it about in a fanatical fashion, bringing down blows with such severity, he cleaved an arm off from one and took the hand off another. The fighting had broken down into a chaotic melee. With bodies and riderless horses all around, and the remains of the powder smoke clinging to them all, the advantages of the horsemen had been heavily nullified.

The Frenchmen still thundered blows down at the infantrymen below, but not one of the Portuguese infantry turned and fled. They fought like lions as they thrust up into the cavalrymen. Many were dragged from their saddles or smashed from them by the butts of muskets. Craven smashed his sabre down into another cavalryman, cleaving into his collar with such tremendous blows as one would expect from Birback, but not the rather more skilful Craven. One cavalryman, seeing Craven cutting through his comrades, drew a pistol and took aim at the Captain. Yet before he could fire, a bayonet lashed across his hand and knocked the pistol from his grasp. The musket was in the hands of Lopo, the man who had fought dirty to win the friendly contest just minutes before all the chaos had begun. He did not play any tricks any longer and levelled his bayonet at the Frenchman, plunging it into the man's chest.

Craven turned sharply as a rider approached at speed, and he saw Paget approaching on a captured horse. His hat was missing, and blood trickled down his face where it looked as though he had been pommelled, and yet he smiled having clearly won the contest to secure the animal. All around them steel clashed. Some of the Portuguese soldiers had picked up the swords of the cavalry and set about them with ferocity. The morale of the French troops was breaking. It had wavered the moment Ferreira shot their commanding officer, and it had gotten worse with every step they advanced and every soldier they lost. Having few officers or even sergeants left to lead them, their will was broken. Paget could see it and pushed on forward, running one of them through before the eyes of many of his comrades. Cries of panic to withdraw rang out.

"They are running, Sir, they're running!" Paget cried excitedly. He swung his sword about his head just as the French officer had done before Ferreira shot him from his horse, but this time it was in triumph and victory.

"See them off, Mr Paget," ordered Craven.

"Follow me!"

The Lieutenant had just six other mounted troops by his side, including Ferreira who happily let him lead the charge.

Craven remained with the infantry, watching the Portuguese troops finish off the last of the French troops who had been unhorsed. One ran for his life but was bayonetted through the back. Nobody had any sympathy for the man. He was an invader, and he came to do just the same to all of them, and in their homeland. The slaughtering was soon over.

Several horses lay dead, and dozens of the French cavalrymen as well as almost as many of the Portuguese infantry. It had been a costly affair for all, but no one was under any illusion as to who had been victorious. A trail of more French dead ran all the way back to the woods from where they had come. Cheers rang out from the Portuguese troops who had won an all or nothing victory. Craven reloaded both barrels of his pistol, as he watched Paget and the others chase the French cavalry who far outnumbered them but dared not turn to fight after such horrifying losses. After reloading, he placed the readied pistol back in his saddle holster and took up the French sabre which he had tucked under his arm whilst loading. He couldn't help but admire the quality.

The aesthetics hurt his eyes and the hilt was overly heavy, resulting in a very hilt balanced sword. It was made worse by the extra weight on one side which caused it to want to pull to one side. A feature only made tolerable by the extensive curve of the blade which encouraged the blade to align as it was swung. He hated the way it looked and felt, but there was no denying it was robust and a sublime cutter. British light cavalry sabres were notorious for their savagery in the cut, and they certainly looked more brutal with their broad hacking tips. Yet the French sabre he had swung like an executioner's blade was no light cutter either. The proof was in the streaks of blood running down the cold steel.

As he looked at it, he spotted his sword out of the corner of his eye. He threw the French sword down, causing it to spear the ground before leaping from his horse. He went to the body of the man who had taken his sword down to the ground embedded in his body. Craven turned the man over to see he was long gone. He pulled the blade from his victim and used the Frenchman's tunic to wipe the blood from the blade. The Portuguese troops looked on at him differently now. Not for what he had done, but for what they had; as if they finally felt worthy of his presence and with some kinship, the sort of brotherhood he and his comrades enjoyed.

"A good day, Sir!" Lopo cried.

"A good day indeed."

Matthys approached with the handful of Salfords he had

by his side. All but Charlie was cut and bleeding. Caffy had a large gaping wound at his shoulder which looked as though it might have dismembered a slighter man. Their uniforms were all cut up. The Sergeant did not celebrate the victory like the Portuguese soldiers did.

The Portuguese troops began to shout Craven's name, celebrating the victory as if it was his alone, and that made Matthys angrier. Craven signalled for them to quieten so that he might address them, and he soon went on.

"Today you defended your country, and you did your countrymen proud. You took a stand in the face of French cavalry and said, no more!"

The crowd loved it, but as the cries died down, Matthys stepped up to say his piece, fuming with anger.

"Do you not see! Would you have each and every one of us fight until there is no man left? Until the Salfords are nothing more than a memory?"

"We did not lose a single soul, did we not?" Craven replied.

"Through sheer luck. For many of us came close, and we could all of us have been one of those men lying dead in the dirt!" He pointed to the men dead because of the Portuguese infantry.

Craven had no words to explain it, nor any excuses, and Matthys soon continued.

"I told you, Craven. We are not the only ones fighting this war. You promised we would go to Lisbon and take our leave. We must get away from this war, at least for a while, or it will consume us all."

"And do they get the same luxury?" Craven pointed to the

Portuguese troops.

"Yes, many times over. A soldier is not made to fight every day. You forget that this is the war, not the gladiatorial arena. We weren't made to keep on fighting without rest. We came here to see a good man honoured, but we are long overdue our return to the city."

"And if we had not been here?" Craven asked as he looked at the results of the bloody battle.

"Someone else would be, or do you think you fight every battle of this war?"

Craven looked to the others to find no support amongst them, not even from Paget, who for all the excitement he had gotten caught up in, had quickly come back down from the adrenaline rush. Every one of them was with Matthys. It was an embarrassment for Craven, and before so many of the troops. He had pushed them all too far, and he knew it, but he'd also been made to look a fool.

"See to the wounded, have burial parties organised, and word sent on of the enemy movements we have encountered here," he ordered.

Matthys looked almost sick for having to stand up to Craven, but there was nothing more to say as he went to render what aid he could. Ferreira sent messengers on to relay the news. Many of the men began to patch up their own wounds or help one another. For a great many had suffered at the whirling and hacking blows of the French sabres. Some were merely superficial whilst many were horrific wounds, but the sort that most soldiers could survive so long as they could fight any infection which might follow. Matthys felt bad for having spoken up so publicly, and after seeing to several wounds, he went to Craven who looked deep in thought.

"I am sorry," he declared.

"It's a little late for that," snarled Craven.

"It's never too late. Something needed to be said."

"But not now, not here, not after a victory. Victory in a battle which could have been the end of us all. You saw what this did to boost their spirits, and you would strip that away from them?" Craven scowled.

"If that is what must be done."

"I didn't come here to fight, but a fight came to us," he replied defensively.

"You stayed out here longer than we needed to, and then you marched out infantry close to the border. Don't tell me you were not hoping for this?" Matthys accused him.

"Of course, I was not!"

But Matthys shook his head, not believing a word of it.

"You've never been a good liar," replied Matthys.

"Get out of my sight!"

Matthys did so gladly, going back to the wounded to give what aid he could.

"He does not mean it, Sir," insisted Paget as he tried to calm all their nerves.

"Yes, he does," snapped Craven.

"What are your orders?" Ferreira asked.

"As soon as we are done here, we ride for Lisbon," he begrudgingly growled, knowing they were all behind Matthys.

CHAPTER 3

Paget listened as Portuguese troops said some words beside the graves of those they had lost. He didn't understand a word of it, but he got the sentiment, although he was more focused on Craven and Matthys and the scathing animosity between the two. It pained Paget to see, and yet he could sympathise with both of them, and could find no way to fix it if they could not see the same. It was a solemn affair as any funeral would be, but it was especially bitter when the day should have been nothing more than a training exercise. It had started out so well and gotten them all in such high spirits. Ferreira's anger with Craven had at least abided, for there were far greater things to be concerned with, and he looked to Paget, showing the same woes which troubled the young Lieutenant. The brotherhood of the Salfords was splitting at the seams, and Paget knew Matthys was correct as to the reasons why. Yet he was with Craven first and foremost, and ultimately saw no reason to rest either. He came to Portugal and Spain to be a soldier, not to lay about idle.

The ceremony came to an end, and the Lieutenant instinctively went to put his hat back on, it having been tucked under his arm. It had slipped his mind as to why he had not been wearing it when all others had, and the bicorne knocked against the bandage wrapped about the crown of his head to stem the bleeding of the wound he had suffered at the pommel of a French sabre. He winced a little but was more angered by his inability to wear his own uniform hat; the bicorne he so vehemently held onto in spite of moving to a shako, which he looked down upon as a common soldier's attire, despite it rapidly becoming the norm for most officers throughout the army. They said their goodbyes to many appreciative Portuguese soldiers, including the two cavalrymen who had sought refuge with them. It was a warming scene, and yet Paget could not help but dwell on Matthys' accusations. He wondered if Craven really had led them close to the dangers of the border in the hope of seeking out a fight with the French. He didn't know how to feel about the possibility. For if Craven had, then the skirmish was not a triumph against the odds, but a foolish risk that cost many lives.

Paget wanted to say something. He wanted to ask more questions, but he could see how tense the situation was between Craven and Matthys and knew he could not utter a word of it without inflaming those tensions further. What's more, he could see Ferreira and the others felt it, too. Only one amongst them seemed oblivious to it, and that was Archie Hunt. Maybe he was just naïve, and maybe he just didn't know them as well as Paget did, but the former Captain of the Portuguese light cavalry looked more than just oblivious, he looked bored. He was a curious stray, hanging onto Craven and the others for some sense of purpose, or perhaps an excuse as to not have to return to his duties. Yet Paget realised he was hardly in a place to complain. For he himself was in a not dissimilar position. Wellington had put him where he was to keep him out of the way, though it made him smile to know that the effect had been quite the opposite.

The small band of Salfords soon said their goodbyes and left with the gratitude of those soldiers who remained at the border, for none of them believed Craven would have led them into danger and saw him as a great champion amongst the army. They rode on, seven riders returning on the road West to Lisbon.

It had taken them a hurried two days to reach the funeral service of Colonel Bevan, but the urgency was now gone, and at leisurely pace it would be three days' ride if not more, but they all welcomed it. For from the border, they were safe from the French, and they could see life was returning to relative normalcy. After the scorched Earth approach on the retreat to the protection of the lines of Torres Vedras, they had seen so much destroyed. Houses burnt down and crops ruined. Anything which might be of value to the enemy was taken away or destroyed in place, but as they rode on, they could see the fields full and the people who worked them had also returned.

It was a heart-warming sight, and yet with a vast French army waiting at the border, it was a deeply uncomfortable one, leaving many feeling as though they relaxed on a cliff edge. They rode on peacefully for an entire day and rested easy in the night, though without the group's usual vigour in conversation. For an anger remained amongst Craven and Matthys the likes of which nobody dared attempt to intervene in. The next day they went on. Paget purposely looked as cheerful as possible, trying to lead the group forward into better spirits, but he faced an uphill battle. And so, he diverted his attentions to Ferreira, for the Captain at least looked neutral in his expression.

"Back to your home city we ride," declared Paget in a friendly tone.

"Yes," grumbled Ferreira.

"That does not bring you joy?"

"Do you think I would have joined the army if I loved my city so much?"

Paget didn't know whether it was cynicism or sarcasm, but he didn't care for it either way.

"Why do you hate your home so much? You hate your city, you hate your countrymen, you hate everything that you were born to, why?" he asked in an accusing fashion.

"Do you love everything about your country without question?"

"Of course, it is why I am here to defend it."

"For what reason? What has kindled that love?"

"All Englishmen are born with it in their hearts."

Ferreira laughed.

"You do not believe it?" Paget demanded.

"What do you think Craven would say?"

Paget shrugged, knowing the Captain would not be so enthusiastic.

"You love England because you were told to, but I believe love must be earned. I do not hate my country nor its people. I merely reserve my love for where it is deserved. When I see my countrymen stand firm and show they are worthy of some pride, it is the greatest thing, and I have seen it, Mr Paget. I have seen men who I had no faith in stand and turn away the best Napoleon has to offer. That is the kind of moment when I will feel love in my heart. Not because it was expected of me, but because it was genuine and worthy."

Paget was stunned as he thought about the sentiment before finally replying.

"Should one not love wholeheartedly, for all that is both good and bad?"

"Why?" Ferreira laughed.

"Duty?"

Once again Ferreira laughed, but Paget was not impressed.

"I do not understand how you can fight for a country you do not love."

"Do you love every officer who has ever commanded you?"

"Well, no, some of them have been foul fellows," he replied quietly, looking around to make sure nobody else would hear him criticise them.

"But you follow their orders all the same?"

"Why, yes, of course."

"And so, you do not love them, but you do follow them."

"Of course."

"Then you have your answer. You do not love everything wholeheartedly, but you know there is enough good that is worth fighting for."

Paget thought about it for a few minutes before shrugging as if unconvinced. To him it sounded all the same.

"I think you have a bleak opinion of your country and its people."

Craven laughed as he came up beside them, and Paget took that as positive reinforcement to continue to his bombardment of the Portuguese Captain.

"Each and every one of us make up what a country is, and so if you want your country to be better, do you not stand with yourself?"

Craven laughed again as he had Ferreira over a barrel, and any attempt to resist Paget's assessment would only prove his point. Yet Ferreira did not look angry but more fascinated by the prospect as he gave it more thought.

"I'd say the Captain has already come a long way from the grumpy layabout he once was. He just forgets sometimes," added Craven.

Ferreira burst out with laughter, seeing the light side of it all. They were in good spirits, all of them except Matthys who was still seething with Craven for the danger he believed he had put them all in and the lives it had cost. It dampened the mood of them all every time it was noticed, and nobody could find the words to heal those wounds. Matthys found little sympathy amongst the rest of them. It was as if even if Craven had put them close to danger in the hope of a fight, none of them would be particularly bothered, having accepted they were there to fight, and many of them even enjoyed it.

"What now, Sir?" Paget asked.

"We were promised leave, and that is what we will get. Some time of peace in Lisbon, far from the French and the chaos," he replied loudly for all to hear, especially Matthys, as if to prove a point that he was always planning to return West for such a purpose. In this few of them were convinced, though, not even Paget, who knew how eager Craven was to fight.

They soon settled in for the night under the stars with only tree coverage as shelter. They were in no rush, and whilst the comforts of a bed were a welcome thought, their bodies were all well-worn, and they welcomed the slow trudge back to Lisbon. As the sun went down, Paget took the first watch, and he had been awake for several hours with only his own mind to keep himself company. He rubbed his eyes as he tried to stay awake. As he looked up, he saw what looked to be a glimmer of movement. He shot up for a better look and his hand reached for his sword grip. There was a tiny flutter of movement in a branch in the distance as a low breeze swept through. He breathed a sigh of relief as he went over to Craven to awaken him to his turn, but to his surprise the Captain was wide awake.

"Is everything okay, Sir?"

"Yes, and with you?"

Paget looked out to where he thought he had seen some movement, distrusting his own weary eyes before shrugging.

"Yes, Sir."

Craven sat up. He clearly had a great weight on his mind, and Paget did not have to ask what the cause of it was, but he was curious about some of the details. He looked especially awkward as if holding his tongue as he took short deep breaths and tried to speak several times before pausing.

"What is it?" Craven asked wearily.

"Sir, about what Matthys said, that you marched those men into danger, looking for trouble, looking for a fight, is it true?" he finally asked.

Craven thought on it for a little while, before sighing as he got up to stretch his legs and take his turn.

"Get some rest." He picked up his sword and made his

way out to make a circuit of their small encampment.

It left Paget feeling uneasy. He could not tell if it was because Craven did not want to admit that Matthys had been right, or he had just been overwhelmed by it all and could not bear to hear anymore. He knew that would not be the end of it. Matthys would not let it go, and Craven was just as stubborn. He settled in for the night as best he could. Despite the squabbles amongst them, he felt relieved to finally be on the road to Lisbon and far from the dangers of the front lines. He felt a sense of achievement and almost that he was going home after the end of a war, or he imagined it was something akin to that experience. He began to reflect on all they had done recently. Th French had been halted at the border. Portugal was kept safe. Some honour was restored to a man who had died in the most awful and unfair of circumstances, and they had even settled the dispute between Hawkshaw and Timmerman, or at least prevented them from killing one another.

With triumphant thoughts on his mind, Paget fell fast asleep, and another day on the road soon followed. Spirits rose a little higher with every step closer to Lisbon, and even Matthys was starting to relax. He would not forget his anger with Craven, but he was beginning to feel foolish for letting it interfere with his duties and the comradery the rest of them had grown so accustomed to. He continued to avoid Craven, but otherwise he was almost back to his usual self. The day went quickly as they reminisced about the years they had served together and all they had seen and done. On reflection, it seemed truly mindboggling and a reminder as to why they needed to reach Lisbon and spend some weeks if not months relaxing and recovering from the hardships they had endured.

At nightfall Paget once again took the first watch, and yet again his exhaustion and lack of anyone to banter with led his eyes to fall heavy. He phased in and out of consciousness, barely staying upright. He heard steps beside him and turned to see Hawkshaw pacing out to the edge of the camp to relieve himself. Paget nodded in acknowledgement before his eye lids began to droop once more.

A glimmer of movement ahead caused him to rise a little and look out just as he had before. He shook his head, thinking himself foolish for being so jumpy, but he spotted movement again and a glimmer of light which did not look natural. A small surge of adrenaline caused his eyes to shoot open, and he could make out the shape of the muzzle of a musket in the trees ahead and a tiny glimmer of moonlight shinning from it. He heard a dull thud and a quiet gasp and looked over to where Hawkshaw had gone. It was dark, but he could make out movement, and it was more than just a single figure. He scooped up his pistol and cocked it ready whilst picking up his sword in its scabbard in readiness. He went toward the commotion. It was quiet and subtle but more than enough to be of serious concern. As he drew closer, he could see two men carrying a third, who looked unconscious. It was Hawkshaw.

"Stop there!"

He lifted his pistol into the air and fired a shot. Knowing he could not risk hitting the Captain, but that the sharp crack of the pistol would be enough to bring the rest of those sleeping to his aid, as if calling on a hunting horn to rally the hunt. The eruption from both the pan and the muzzle of his small pistol were enough to light up the entire area for a brief moment, and he could see a dozen more figures lurking in the treeline with muskets, pistols, and swords. They wore no uniforms, but they were extremely well armed. Those carrying the Captain hurried on, but Charlie leapt up beside Paget and quickly assessed what she was seeing, being wide awake at the crack of gunfire.

"They're taking Captain Hawkshaw!" Paget cried for all to hear as the others rushed onto the scene.

Charlie took aim at the two men carrying him without the hesitation Paget had shown. She fired and put a rifle ball into the chest of one, causing all three of the men to crash down to the ground. Matthys was up next with rifle in hand. The embers of powder and wadding from Charlie's shot quickly caught on the bone-dry foliage ahead of them and suddenly lit up the scene, revealing the true extent of what they were facing. At least twenty well-armed men. Matthys did not wait any longer as he shouldered his rifle and took aim at a man rushing to Hawkshaw to help carry him away in place of the one who had been shot dead.

The flash of burning powder from Matthys' rifle lit up the scene further, and Craven's eyes opened wide in horror at what they were facing. He fired his pistol, and more shots rang out from those beside him, but they soon fell silent as they had so little firepower. The small band rushed forward with blades as the fire spread and lit the scene well. Several armed men ran toward Hawkshaw but did not fire, using the butts of their muskets and the swords in their hands.

Craven waded into them, smashing one in the mouth with the butt of his heavy pistol and knocking several teeth out before cutting down at another. His blade was beaten aside by a musket. Paget thrust into the shoulder of one who was trying to drag Hawkshaw on, and in no time at all they had surrounded the unconscious Captain. Steel clashed, but they were soon at a stalemate as the rogues backed off, realising they would not get near their target.

"Come on, come on, you bastards!" Hunt cried.

But the men backed away, and Hunt moved to pursue.

"Leave them!" Craven roared.

He knew they could not risk going too far from Hawkshaw who had still not come around. Craven watched their attackers back away with great suspicion. He looked for anything which might identify them, but there was nothing. They had not even spoken a word with which they might be identified from language or accent. In no time at all they had vanished into the night, and the fire was giving little visibility. Matthys and Caffy retrieved their blankets and began to beat out the fire until once again darkness fell over the sight. The enemy had left their dead behind but nothing more and were nowhere to be seen.

"What the hell was that?" Hunt demanded.

"Bouchard's vipers?" Paget asked.

Craven shook his head. "They would not hold their fire."

"These men came with one purpose," replied Matthys as he supported Hawkshaw's head whilst he regained consciousness.

"But why?"

Craven looked at the dead.

"British muskets. British swords."

"Then they are our own men, Sir?"

"Supplied with British weapons doesn't mean they are British," replied Matthys.

"Hawkshaw has but one enemy," seethed Craven.

"You don't think?" Charlie asked.

"Of course, I do. These were no common bandits."

For a moment Matthys forgot his woes with Craven in light of one of their own being in danger. "We can't prove it."

"We don't need to," replied Craven scathingly.

"He would dare attack us, Sir?"

"Attack? No. These men were not permitted to do us harm. They did not even fire their muskets. They waited for their moment to take Hawkshaw from under our noses as if he merely walked off into the night and vanished."

"How could they manage it? Who was on watch?" Ferreira asked.

"I was," replied Paget.

"Explain to me exactly what happened."

"The Captain got up in the night to relieve himself on the edge of the camp, and the next thing I heard was a commotion. Upon investigation, I discovered men carrying the Captain away."

"Then they were watching us and waiting. Waiting for the perfect moment to strike," replied Matthys.

"I…I…" stuttered Paget.

"What is it?" Craven demanded.

"A night previously, Sir, I thought I saw something in the woods."

"Why the hell didn't you say anything?"

"I was tired, I wasn't sure, I didn't think…"

"No, you did not! The next time you think you saw something which might endanger our lives, you report it!"

Paget slumped. He looked pale and forlorn, like a puppy who had just been disciplined.

"You've got to admire Timmerman's balls to try and pull

this off," admitted Charlie.

But Craven shook his head as he knew it was far from over.

"Three on watch at all times and be ready for anything. In the morning we ride with all haste!" he snapped as he began to reload his double-barrelled pistol.

CHAPTER 4

Both men and horses were tired when Craven's party reached the edge of Lisbon as the sun was going down. They had ridden hard all day so as to not have to spend another night out in the wilderness being stalked by whoever came after them. The experience of the previous night left them all with many questions. It was a mysterious force that had attacked them, but a well-disciplined one, not even firing a shot despite being fired upon. They were all tired and many also bloodied and bruised from the encounter with the French cavalry. They needed the protection of the city, and more importantly, the protection of their own comrades, the Salford Rifles.

It felt like they were running away, but to have such a dangerous mysterious force looming over them was scary even if none of them would admit it. There was not one amongst them who did not have a sore neck from continually looking over their shoulder all the way to Lisbon. It was made all the worse by the scathing expressions they received from a number of officers as they rode on into the city, as if they were somehow the enemy. The Portuguese militia welcomed them as heroes, but many British officers looked upon them with disgust.

"Why do they look at us so, Sir?" Paget asked Ferreira.

"I have no idea," sighed Craven.

They had only been gone a couple of weeks, and they had left in good spirits, but something had changed, and that made them all feel more anxious. They had come to Lisbon to seek comfort and refuge, and it was starting to feel like they would have neither. Craven tried to shrug it off as if they were overthinking it, for a great many officers had hated him his entire life. But it was hard to not feel paranoid when gangs of well-armed men were hunting you in the night.

It was not long before they reached the bar, which was both their watering hole and also billets for all who had travelled with Craven. They stepped inside to a cheer from several dozen of the Salfords who were drinking inside. It was a relief to them all to finally be made welcome and be surrounded by the safety of their own comrades, though Lieutenant Gamboa approached them with concern at the sight of their condition.

"You found trouble on at the border?"

"Yes, and on the road back," admitted Craven.

"Bandits?"

"Not the kind I have ever encountered," replied Craven as he pushed his way through to the bar where he was relieved to be passed a drink without having to ask for it. Gamboa turned his attention to Ferreira, hoping to get some answers.

"What is the Captain talking about?"

"The French cavalry need no explanation, but the men

who came after us whilst we slept just one day's ride from here, they did not come to kill us."

"Then what?" Gamboa pressed for an explanation.

"They came for Captain Hawkshaw, and they wanted him alive."

Quental sighed as he joined them.

"I fear there is a lot more at work here," he admitted.

"What do you mean?" Ferreira demanded.

"There is talk amongst some of the officers."

"What talk?"

"Some say Colonel Bevan was a coward who killed himself because of his own failings."

"And?"

"They say Captain Craven championed the cause of a coward who let a whole French garrison escape."

"And why should that matter?"

"Because the sentiment by some officers is far from positive towards Captain Craven, and you know it," added Gamboa.

Ferreira knew it to be true, for a great many despised Craven for being the rogue that he was. They despised his lack of manners and discipline and respect for authority, and more than anything, they hated how much Wellington seemed to admire him, or at least that was what many said, despite the fiery encounters the two often shared.

"What matter is it of ours? These are rumours, none of it matters."

"Of course, it matters," added Matthys as he joined them.

"Why should it? We are unstoppable," replied Gamboa.

"Unstoppable because we have an army at our backs, and

what if that army is no longer there?"

"What are you saying?"

"That we rely on one another, and if we have lost the respect and support of the army, then we are in big trouble."

"We don't know that is the case," insisted Ferreira.

They watched as Craven raised several glasses and made toasts to rampant cheers, but to the officers who knew better, there was nothing to celebrate.

Ferreira picked up his rifle as he went for the door.

"Where are you going?" Quental asked.

"I must know more."

"It can wait a day, can it not? You have only just arrived, and all of you look as though you have been through much."

"That does not change the facts. We are under attack."

"Not here you are not. You are safe here, you are amongst brothers," insisted Gamboa.

"And when night falls and most are drunk or asleep? Or the next time we must go somewhere without the protection of all of this?"

"I am sure Craven has it handled," insisted Quental.

Matthys huffed and said nothing, but it was enough to cause concern amongst them all.

"Should we not inform Captain Craven of what you are doing?" Gamboa asked.

Ferreira took once last glance at the Captain. He looked far too busy taking his fill of drinks and trying to forget all of their problems. Ferreira shook his head.

"I am going with you," declared Quental.

"So am I," Gamboa added.

Barros nodded in agreement as well. The three officers

and one Sergeant comprised most of the senior command staff of the Portuguese element of the Salfords, which was also most of the unit these days.

"You should take some of the men with you for protection," declared Matthys.

"We can protect ourselves. You keep an eye on Hawkshaw." He looked forwards to the Captain who was slumped in a chair with a blank expression, as if still feeling the effects of a severe concussion. He barely knew where he was or why.

"I will make sure no ill comes of the Captain, or at least nothing beyond liquor," he sighed.

Ferreira nodded in gratitude and headed out the door. Upon reaching the street, he slung his rifle onto his shoulder and adjusted his sword belt. He lifted one of the scabbard hanging loops onto the hook of his belt so that the sword clung there and could be readily and quickly drawn with just one hand.

"Are you expecting trouble?" Quental asked.

"No, but I should be ready for it either way," he admitted.

But the truth was he did expect to find men waiting for them, even within the relative safety of the city.

"Come on," he growled as he led them on.

They soon received several more scathing glances from passing junior British officers. They could not tell whether it was because of the Portuguese uniforms worn by three of them or because they were recognised as being Craven's men. Either way it was an unsettling sight.

"Surely the whole city cannot have turned on Captain Craven, not after all he has done for Lisbon?" Gamboa asked.

"The inhabitants, no, but those are not the ones we have

to worry about."

"How bad is it?" Barros asked Quental.

"I don't know. I thought it was just idle chatter, and until I heard of the attack on the Captain's encampment, I did not think anything of it."

"If this really is Timmerman's work, then he has really upped his game," replied Ferreira.

"How so?"

"He used to just come right at us with fire and fury, but now he expands his strategies, if indeed it is the work of Timmerman."

"What will we do?" asked Quental.

"The first thing is we need information."

He said nothing, but they all knew where he was leading them as they turned the hill to Lady Sarmento's home. It brought memories flooding back for all of them, many of them bad ones that had brought them all close to death. Ferreira stormed up the hill and smashed heavily on the Lady's door and showed no patience in repeating the action just seconds later. Finally, the door opened, and they were greeted by Tuma.

"Good evening, gentlemen."

"Is the Lady in?"

"She is presently entertaining several guests, Sir."

Ferreira shoved the door open and pushed his way in. Tuma did not resist but looked rather flustered. Ferreira raced on through in a scene reminiscent of Timmerman when he had barrelled into the house in much the same way. It brought back some painful memories, and he could not help but feel he was repeating the series of events, and yet he was too impatient to wait. He turned the bend into the dining room to find the Lady sitting with two other women and three British officers, being two Majors and a Colonel. They looked most put out by the unwelcome guest, and even more so when they caught sight of his Portuguese uniform. The table was amassed with food, the quantities the likes of which a common soldier could only dream of, and not one of them looked as though they had seen any harm in the wars. Their uniforms were impeccable, and they bore no scars nor even tanned skin from any time in the field.

"What is the meaning of this?" demanded the Colonel.

The Lady looked initially scared, likely also remembering Timmerman's arrival, but she looked even more uncomfortable when she saw that it was in fact Ferreira.

"My apologies, Colonel, but these men do not know their manners." She stood up to usher them back to the lobby, but the Colonel soon piped up.

"You, you are one of Craven's fellows, aren't you?"

"Yes," sighed Ferreira, as the name was not finding them any good will elsewhere at present.

"The men who rallied behind a coward and tried to defend that coward before Wellington. I hear you even rode to his funeral to blubber further."

The two Majors laughed profusely.

"Well, are you not?" pressed the Colonel.

"Yes, Captain Ferreira," he sighed again.

"Ah, Craven's Portuguese dog."

Quental tried to press forward angrily, but Ferreira held him back, and the others knew better than to cause trouble.

"You see, all bark and no bite," smiled the Colonel, drawing more laughs from the Majors. Craven looked furious, and Ferreira could not let it stand. He took a deep breath and replied calmly.

"Which fields of battle might I have recognised you fine gentlemen? Were you at Talavera? Bussaco? Sabugal? Perhaps at Fuentes de Oñoro?"

The room was silent, and Quental could not help but smile.

"Because we were there. We were there fighting the French face to face time and time again. A dog, you say? I'd rather be a dog fighting in the pits than an idle fat pig."

The Colonel shot up angrily up, launching his chair back into the wall behind him, but Lady Sarmento also shot up and rushed between them.

"Excuse me, gentlemen, but this is no place for such behaviour."

"Yes, quite," replied the Colonel. He sat back down rather more calmly as a servant lifted his chair for him.

"I would say your commanding officer will hear of this, but you do not even have such a man, do you?" he scathingly replied to Ferreira.

"I am sure Lord Wellington will be more than happy to hear your complaints," replied Ferreira with a straight face.

"Get out of my sight!"

The Lady Sarmento led them away and back into the lobby. She looked quite flustered.

"You would entertain those disgusting creatures?"

"Of course, for that is what I must do. Do I need to remind you it is for men like that we even still have a country left?"

Ferreira grumbled, knowing it were true.

"What is happening here, Ma'am?" Gamboa asked.

"It is as I feared," Quental said.

Lady Sarmento nodded in agreement.

"Major Timmerman has much money and influence, and he has used both freely to tarnish the name of Craven and all of you, and it is hardly difficult when you supported a coward. A man who killed himself because he could not accept ridicule for his own failures."

"That is not what happened. Bevan was no coward," replied Ferreira solemnly.

"It doesn't matter anymore. He is dead, and nothing will change that, but you insist on making it worse by taking his side."

"Because it is the right thing to do."

"The right thing?" She paused for a moment before laughing, barely holding back tears at the same time. She then whispered to him, "Do you even know what the right thing is?"

Ferreira looked confused.

"Do you think I want to entertain those pigs in there? They are no better than Major Timmerman, and I have seen plenty more like him in these past weeks also. Don't talk to me about what is right. You talk with the piety of a bishop and yet you do it all for your own pride. I wish I had the same luxury many days."

"Don't you? You live in these fine houses with everything you could ever want and go and do as you please, not a day of work in sight."

She slapped him hard across the face with such force as it struck more like a punch. He was stunned by it.

"I am fighting this war in every way that I can. Do not dare speak to me in such a way!"

The three British officers stormed into the room having heard the slap of Ferreira's cheek and rushed to give some assistance.

"Is everything okay?"

"Yes, Colonel, Captain Ferreira was just leaving."

The Colonel initially looked suspicious, but then he caught a glimpse of Ferreira's cheek which was red and had already started to swell. He smirked before laughing as he led the other two back to the table.

"Good evening, Captain!" he replied mockingly to another roar of laughter from the two others.

Ferreira was seething. He did not even know their names, but he wanted to draw their blood.

"Go, for I am already out of favour with many, and the longer you stay the worse it gets," said Lady Sarmento.

"I wouldn't want to inconvenience you," he seethed.

Lady Sarmento felt awful, but she could not say or do anything to help as she ushered them out of the door. Ferreira watched as it closed behind them, leaving them out on the street, having gained nothing of any use, confirming all that Quental had already told him.

"How can you let them talk to you like that?" Gamboa asked.

"What could he do?" replied Quental.

"Nothing good," admitted Ferreira as he clearly thought about demanding satisfaction, even though he was really in no position to do so, for a Colonel would not need to pay him any notice.

"And Lady Sarmento? Where was she when we needed her?" Quental asked.

"She is trying to survive just like the rest of us."

"I don't see her out on the battlefield with musket balls whistling past her face."

"She's seen more than her fair share," admitted Ferreira.

But Quental wasn't satisfied, and Ferreira felt compelled to defend her after all she had done for them.

"Ostracisation to someone like that is as good as death to many others."

But the door to the house opened briefly again, and Tuma stepped out to address them quietly.

"I am sorry," he admitted, having been ashamed by the action of the Lady's guests but having no power to intervene.

Ferreira could sympathize.

"Timmerman was here again?"

"Yes, Sir, several times."

"Did he harm her?"

"No, Sir, but he is most intimidating."

"What did he want?"

"To know more about Captain Hawkshaw and where he might be."

"What did the Lady tell him?"

"Nothing, for she could not help, but I do not believe that she would even if she did know something," he said in her support.

Ferreira nodded in agreement, despite sighing in frustration. He had hoped to find a useful ally, not a voiceless pawn held hostage by her own reputation and standing, but he understood why.

"It is as if Timmerman has turned the city against us, all over a dispute with a single man," he declared.

"Yes, Sir, the Major has made it his mission to discredit your regiment."

"Why? Why all of us?" replied Gamboa.

"Because he will do anything to get what he wants, no matter how low he must stoop nor how much damage he must cause," replied Ferreira.

"I thought the Major was an ally. A difficult one yes, but an ally nonetheless."

"Sometimes, but that man is whatever he wants to be whenever it suits him."

"But he would truly set the whole city upon us just for revenge upon one man?"

"Damn right he would. He would do it just fun, but in this case, he has a reason, doesn't he?"

"But why would officers of the army turn on Craven so easily?"

Ferreira had some ideas, but he looked to Tuma, knowing he would have the latest gossip, having stood beside many dinner tables as drunken officers aired their woes with one another without any restraint or care at all.

"Many men do not like the Captain's flamboyance, nor his lack of discipline, but in all honesty, what they despise most is that he gets results whilst not really being one of them. They despise him for it."

Ferreira patted Tuma on the back. He was a smart and perceptive man.

"Thank you, I appreciate it," he declared, knowing he took many risks coming to speak with them.

He left them in a frustrated state as Ferreira went back down the hill. A passing group of militiamen saluted and greeted them with pleasantries, but a British Lieutenant spat on the ground beside them as he passed.

Barros turned as if to go after the man, but Ferreira grabbed him by the collar to hold him back.

"That's right, keep your dog back!" yelled the officer before laughing as he went on with two other young officers.

"Do not start trouble here," insisted Ferreira.

"They speak to us like we are nothing. What have they ever done? They are probably fresh off the boat. I doubt they've ever even seen a Frenchman or tasted the fog of a volley," snarled Barros.

Ferreira sighed in frustration as he felt it, too, but he struggled to find any answers.

"How quickly people can forget," lamented Gamboa.

"What now?" Quental asked.

Ferreira struggled to find any answers.

"I thought this feud between Hawkshaw and Timmerman was done, at least for a while, but if he will not let it go, then we have big trouble on our hands."

"Then what can we do?" Quental pressed.

"I don't know, but I do know one thing, we need Craven on our side. He needs to know all of this, and he needs to act, in one way or another."

"Are you sure that is a good idea? He could tear this city apart," replied Gamboa.

Ferreira smiled as he knew it were true. Craven was no more subtle than Timmerman.

"What is happening here puts us all in danger, and Craven must know of it."

"And what do you think he will do?" Quental asked.

"I don't know, but Timmerman must be dealt with. We cannot have the whole army against us."

He stormed on back towards the bar. It had been an uncomfortable evening so far but not a wholly unfruitful one. At least he now had some inkling as to what they were dealing with and why. Yet as he walked on through the streets, he continually shook his head in anger and frustration. They had come back to Lisbon for rest and felt they had more than earned it, but now the city felt as hostile to them as the front lines.

Several more passers-by groaned and muttered under their breath.

"Timmerman has to go," growled Quental.

"And you would be the one to do it?"

"If necessary."

"And what do you think would happen to you, if you struck down a British major?"

"No one ever needs to know. A man like that should be beaten in his sleep and tossed into the sea."

Ferreira laughed as he nodded in agreement.

"If only that were possible," he smirked.

They soon reached the bar. It was a hive of activity and could be heard from several streets away, the soldiers inside partying as if the war were over. They stepped inside to find Craven and the others in great spirits, shouting out across the room and laughing. Many of them had gathered around a table where Birback and Caffy were in a deadlock of an arm wrestle. Neither man was able to move the other, and the crowd cheered on passionately. None of them seemed to have a care in the world as Ferreira pushed his way through to Craven who was pouring himself more wine.

"We need to talk," insisted Ferreira.

"No, we need to drink!" Craven threw back a glass and quickly went about pouring another.

Ferreira angrily snatched the bottle from his hands, causing some to spill over the table.

"What is it?" Craven snatched the bottle from Ferreira once more.

"The city has turned on us, or at least the British officers stationed here have."

"What's new?" Craven snorted.

"You know this is important. Timmerman has poisoned the well and painted targets on all our backs."

"Let him do what he must." Craven downed another glass and began to sway a little from drunkenness.

"Something must be done!"

"Then go and do it!" Craven walked away with the glass and bottle, not wanting to hear anymore from him.

Those who had travelled to Lady Sarmento's gathered around, fearing the worst.

"Nothing will be fixed this way," declared Quental.

Ferreira agreed and looked towards Hawkshaw. He still looked dazed and yet was sipping away on plenty of wine.

"We cannot force them to help themselves," admitted Ferreira.

CHAPTER 5

A thunderous hammer bashed onto Craven's skull, or at least that is what it felt like as his eyes opened. He winced and reached for his head as if to hold it together before the pulsating caused an eruption. But as he cupped his ears, he realised the inculcating crashing did not originate from within his own head, despite the massive hangover and dehydration he felt. He rolled over in his bed to get a look at the door to his room. It was rattling on its hinges as it was violently beaten upon from someone in the corridor, and now he could hear his voice being called. He slid out of bed, wearing only his shirt and trousers which were unbuttoned where he had clearly collapsed into a deep sleep before he could get them off. He picked up his pistol and went for the door and pulled it open, presenting the muzzle casually forward in case anyone came to do him harm. Though in truth he was in no state to respond in time as his vision was blurred, and he could barely stand, for he was not even fully awake yet and was in a ruinous state.

"It's only me," smiled Hunt with his hands up in a mock surrender.

"What do you want?" Craven hissed.

"Well, there is a nice young man who would like to see you."

"Who?" Craven groaned.

"I have no idea, and I should say he is not all that nice either, at least not in his manners," smirked Hunt.

"It's too early for games, Archie." Craven headed back towards his bed and tossed his pistol down on the dresser.

"It's gone noon," replied Hunt as Craven slumped back onto his bed, groaning at the realisation he needed to get back up. He was regretting the vast quantities of wine and yet already thought of finding some more.

"I think they want to fight you," smiled Archie.

"They? You said there was only one."

"Well, one of them said he wants to fight you, but I would say from the motions of his friends they may also want to."

Craven seemed to wake from the dead as he rose up as if to face the challenge head on.

"A fight, you say?" He tucked his shirt in and buttoned up his trousers, yet his voice was coarse. Hunt handed him a water bottle to help quench his thirst. He took it gladly and took a large gulp only for his eyes to widen with surprise as he struggled to swallow it down.

"That's wine."

"Of course, it is," smiled Hunt.

Craven shook his head in disbelief, as that was extreme even for him.

"You would have me fight drunk?"

"I wouldn't want to make it too easy for you, or it would be no fun," chuckled Hunt.

But Craven thrust the bottle back into his hands, for it was a step too far even though he was tempted to go on and indulge the Captain. Footsteps rang out in the corridor as someone approached at speed. They were light-footed and could not have been drinking a lot the night before. Craven quickly snatched up his pistol once more. He was starting to feel more awake and alert, which made him less lethargic but also more aware of his pounding headache. It now felt almost as bad as the hammering on the door only minutes before.

He carried with him a jug of water, and Craven had never looked so appreciative, knowing the young Lieutenant would never be such a trickster as Hunt. He took the jug and drank from it without even a cup, finishing it off in one. Paget looked relieved to have done something good after the scolding he had received following their ambush. Worst of all he knew he deserved it, and that made him feel even worse. Being a disappointment was a worse prospect than death to him.

The water invigorated Craven further to the extent he was almost his usual self, as if he was able to shrug off the hangover with ease, which he could, for he had much experience at it.

"These young officers come looking for a fight, Sir," said Paget with concern.

"Then they shall have it," smiled Craven.

"You would duel with them, Sir?" Paget was horrified at the prospect.

"That is rather up to them. I have no quarrel with them. I do not even know them."

"But, Sir, after Wellington…"

"Wellington is not here, and there is nothing wrong with a little competition."

"But if someone was to be killed, Sir?"

Duelling was heavily frowned upon but rarely brought much punishment, except in cases where it led to death or an officer's inability to conduct his duty. And Paget could hardly imagine a situation where Craven would let any man off so lightly as for it to not gain the attention of the provosts and even Wellington himself. Paget remembered well how Craven fighting a duel started a great avalanche which brought them all together and made the Salfords what they were today. And yet he knew that was quite by chance, and the duel which began it all was not to be celebrated. He did whatever he could to keep Craven away from any more duels, but he knew he could only do so much.

"Sir, the word about the city is that we are out of favour," he went on.

"What of it?"

"Perhaps drawing the blood of our allies will not help."

"And perhaps those with big mouths would do well to be taught a few lessons."

"I do not believe anybody doubts your ability to fight, Sir," replied Paget almost apologetically for making it sound like they might.

"Then what? What is their problem this day?"

Craven could remember nothing of the night before. He could not remember Ferreira coming to him with his concerns. He barely even remembered entering Lisbon, and so expected a relaxing few days.

"They say we supported a coward," muttered Paget.

"Do they?" Craven answered angrily, for he still felt disgust for the events surrounding Colonel Bevan's death and was sickened to hear him called as such.

"Yes, Sir. Timmerman has poisoned our compatriots against us, Sir. I hear it all over. Some hate you out of jealousy, and others merely because they were told to."

"What has happened here? We were gone for two weeks, and this is what I come back to?"

Ferreira appeared at the doorway trying to hide his frustrations, having explained all of this the night before.

"You knew this would be a risk. Colonel Bevan is a stain on the reputation of this army, and you stood by him even after everything. You could not let it go. A man who was dead and buried and could do no more harm."

"And if it was you in the ground and with such a tarnished name, what would you have me do?"

"Whatever you must to move forward. I wouldn't care because I would be dead."

But Craven shook his head.

"I do not believe it, and neither do you."

Ferreira shrugged, but Craven knew how important his legacy was to him. He always tried to hide the love he had found for the army and for duty, but it shone through no matter how much he tried to maintain his blasé attitude.

"Either way, we have big problems. Timmerman seems to have gotten half the officers in Lisbon to hate us, and specifically to hate you. He is doing everything in his power to weaken us so he may get his hands on your brother."

"I can't stop him from talking, but I can meet this head

on."

"And you think fighting will fix it?"

"That's worked pretty well for me so far," smiled Craven.

Ferreira was not convinced, and Paget looked equally concerned, for they both knew how bad the situation had become. Craven slipped into his jacket and took his sword belt in his hand, without bothering to buckle it to his waist nor button up his jacket. He strolled down the stairs and out into the street where three British officers were awaiting him. They were all quite young and fresh-faced, eager to prove themselves. They stuck out their chests and stretched out as tall as they could, imagining themselves as giants amongst men. Craven smiled as he had seen so many hundreds just like them before, maybe even thousands.

"Captain Craven?" demanded one of them in a curt voice and a very posh and well-educated accent. He could only have come from money, and none of them would be surprised to hear that he had some sort of title.

"At your service."

"You bring dishonour to this army and to England, and I shall have your blood for it!" roared the young man angrily.

"You would die over some rumour you heard?"

"You are no true Englishman, Captain, and I would have you know your place, in the gutter!"

Craven looked to Ferreira and Paget. He shrugged as if to show he had no choice, but it was all a game to him.

"Don't kill him, Sir, for we shall never hear the end of it!!" Paget yelled.

The angry officer seemed to take it as a joke.

"Would you know the name of the man who is about to

humble you?" he said to Craven.

"No, I wouldn't remember it anyway," replied Craven coldly as they drew their swords to fight in the street without any concern for the rules of the duel.

A small crowd had gathered. Some were Salfords whilst others were Royal Navy sailors that had stopped to watch the spectacle, and even local militia whose job it was to enforce the peace. Yet they watched the entertainment like everybody else. The two men began to circle one another, the tips of their swords touching at their maximum reach. The officer carried the same regulation infantry hilt as Craven, but with the common single edged and fullered blade as was most commonly found mated to it.

Craven pressed his own blade more strongly against his opponent's and smiled as he saw it flex excessively under pressure. It was the kind of overly flexible and light blade which had been the death of many users of such a sword. For every officer purchased his own sword, and not all knew the best attributes of such a weapon. Many went to war with weapons only suitable for parade and not up to the task of war. Such an overly flexible blade would struggle to make a good cut as it flexed and wobbled on impact. Even the thrust could be hard to land well, as a uniform jacket could be enough to stop anything but a very straight thrust. The flexibility would let the blade bend as though it were a foil.

As the two men circled, Matthys appeared at the doorway of the bar. Craven looked surprised to see him there, and even more so to catch his gaze, for the Sergeant and old friend had avoided him for days. There was a pleading look in his eyes, begging him to not bring death to the streets that day. Craven nodded in agreement, making a promise with his eyes. The two still did not see eye to eye, but this was more important than any of that, as there was even more at stake now. Craven gave a very slight nod in acknowledgement of the fact.

"What are you waiting for?" Craven's opponent demanded.

"You came here to fight me. Well? Fight me."

The officer launched a quick cut towards his leg. There was speed and skill in the reach of his body and even in his form, but it was the opening action of an amateur. He had done nothing to set it up, nothing which would make it a safe strike to attempt. His head and arm were there and ripe for the taking, but Craven merely slipped the leg out of the way so that he was not struck whilst offering nothing in return. His opponent's comrades cheered with success as if their man had gotten something over Craven. The truth was he could have ended the fight there and then with a simple cut or thrust onto the man's head, who had no means of defending it. Craven wanted to say something, to give the man some lessons, and he could hold his tongue no further.

"Would you attack a Frenchman like that? He'd have had your head clean off."

"And yet you did not," smiled the officer, thinking he was doing a lot better than he really was.

Craven sighed as if dealing with an insolent school child.

"School him!" Hunt shouted.

It didn't help. The officer attacked Craven again. Firstly, with two quick testing cuts and then finally a thrust after he had gotten comfortable. Craven nimbly parried the blade before stepping in and grabbing hold of his opponent's sword hilt. He then ripped it from his grasp. The officer looked furious as if about to protest that Craven had broken the honourable rules of the duel, but he held his tongue, knowing he would look foolish. For this was no smallsword duel between gentlemen. It was a battle between soldiers. Craven tossed the man's sword back to him, which to his credit he caught well. Yet the young man did not seem to have learnt anything from his initial passes against Craven. He just seemed angrier than before, rather than restrained and careful as any competent fighter should be in the face of such a dangerous foe.

"You came to kill me, did you?"

"Why else would I be here?" snarled the young man.

"I just imagined a sober man would think before acting so brashly. Do you even know what you are fighting for?"

Matthys perked up, surprised to hear such words from the Captain, amazed that he was trying to de-escalate the situation, and perhaps save the man's life. But his words had the opposite effect, and the officer came forward angrily, swinging wildly as if he were a cavalryman cutting down fleeing infantryman. Craven parried some blows and merely turned and leaned out of others, the blade passing within a few inches of his body but never close enough to do him harm. It was a miserable display for the young officer who was being humiliated before his friends and before a large crowd. And that made him angrier and even more aggressive, despite how counter-productive that would be, but only a well-trained fighter would know it. Craven did not even offer any attacks of his own until he was backed up close to a line of Royal Navy sailors. He nimbly ducked out of a cut and turned about his opponent, slapping him on the buttocks with the flat of his blade. The officer tried to pretend it had not happened, but his sudden taut response caused laughter from the sailors who had a great view of it all.

"Fight me!" cried the angry officer.

But Craven simply smiled as he was having too much fun.

"Or do you not fight, like that disgraced coward Bevan?"

Craven's smile vanished.

"That bothers you, does it? A shame it did not bother him enough to do his duty and not hide like a frightened little schoolboy before blowing his brains out because he had no honour nor courage!" added the officer, rubbing salt into the wound after seeing how much of a nerve that he had touched the first time.

Craven stepped closer into distance and pressed on the man's blade again, testing to see if it truly was as wobbly as he had first thought. It was, and not only that, but the young officer held a very open and supple grip as if it were a smallsword. Perfect for agile work, but not without some weaknesses. Satisfied that it was as a soft spring, he beat his blade against it, caused it to wobble violently, and resulted in a giggle from the crowd. But Craven watched the blade bow and flex, timing his next move perfectly.

He beat his sword against it again even more violently as the spring bowed in and flexed back against his strike, causing the blade to rebound at speed. The whole sword was catapulted out of the officer's hands and thrown several feet to the ground. The owner looked horrified as he rushed to pick it up, but as he got his hand to the grip, he found the blade pinned to the ground by Craven's foot and the tip of the Captain's sword resting against his chin. He looked stunned but also scared as Craven raised the point and forced him to rise to his feet if not to have his chin cut, abandoning his sword in the process.

"You would strike an unarmed man?" There was fear in his voice.

"I am a man without honour, remember?"

The man gulped in horror as if imagining he was about to have his throat cut.

"Leave, and don't let me see you again!"

The officer breathed a sigh of relief as he looked to his friends, ashamed but also glad to have it all be over. He stepped away from Craven's blade and once again reached down for his own sword.

"Leave it!" Craven roared.

The young man looked horrified but dared not argue as he turned and fled to a roar of laughter from the crowd. Craven turned back to see if he had Matthys' approval, but the Sergeant had already left the scene and returned to the bar.

"Must you have kept his sword also? Must you humiliate the man so completely?" Paget asked as if imagining he could have been that same naive officer not so long ago.

"And what lesson would he learn without punishment?"

"Was a humiliating defeat not enough?"

Craven said nothing but that in itself was an answer. Paget watched the humiliated officer scurry away and felt sorry for him.

"Paget? Are you coming or not?"

Paget realised he had not been listening nor paying attention and looked back in surprise.

"Where, Sir?"

"For a damned walk like I just told you," he replied as he led the way.

"Yes, Sir, of course."

They walked on with Ferreira, Barros, and several of their men alongside them as a squad of bodyguards. Craven didn't much care for the chaperones, but he did not say anything. They strolled on through the streets as if they owned them, and the foul looks were far less frequent now that they had Craven at their head. For many officers knew not to mess with him, no matter how much they disliked him.

They walked on for some time, and despite the heat the fresh air and movement was doing Craven a lot of good. They climbed up to a viewpoint that gave a magnificent view out across the bustling city. He led them to a wooden fence which looked down into the streets below. Not only could they see much of the city from the height, but also the estuary where the busy docks were filled with square rig sail ships as well as wine barges. Naval vessels bristling with guns came and went, but the vast transports were by far the most prevalent. Supplies of everything a great army was needed was shipping in from abroad, for near everything which must be manufactured was still made in Britain or various colonies. It was the kind of machine of war Napoleon could only dream of. He had the vast armies and all the resources of Europe, for which he now controlled almost all of it, but without control over the seas he faced a logistical nightmare.

"We might fight this war on the land, but it is there that the war will be won," declared Craven as he mused on the prospect.

"Yes, so I keep getting told, but I do not see sailors fighting on the battlefield," replied Ferreira.

"They won their great victory at Trafalgar. If only we

could win such a decisive victory on the land," lamented Paget.

"Captain Craven!"

Craven sighed as he turned around half-expecting to find the same man who had come to fight him make a second attempt. To his surprise he did not recognise the man and his associates, but it was a scene remarkably reminiscent of the fight earlier that day. This time there were five of them, all officers, two of them captains, two lieutenants, and an ensign.

"Yes?"

"You dishonour England and this entire army!"

"Here we go again," muttered Ferreira.

Paget looked even more frustrated and yet he said nothing.

"What are you going to do about it?" Craven answered him, without any care for trying to avoid a fight, for he knew there was not a thing he could say that would prevent it.

"I will have blood, and if I am the first to draw it, you will resign your commission and return to England, never to wear the King's uniform again!"

"And if your blood flows first?"

"It will not."

Craven smiled as he took off his jacket in acceptance and finding the whole situation amusing. He handed his sword belt and jacket to Paget before pacing forward to meet the officer, not even pausing to know his name, for it did not matter. The two blades touched, and his opponent wasted no time in getting stuck in. He thrust forward with a deep lunge, plunging towards Craven's chest. He didn't just mean to draw blood, he meant to pierce Craven's heart.

Yet Craven took it all in his stride and parried it away, moving fluidly and calmly as if they fought with only sticks.

Many fighters became anxious in a real fight, especially a duel. Darting back and forth and forgetting all they knew, staying at distance, and desperately hoping to land a strike at the full extension of their reach without risking their own bodies. Yet neither man was that sort here, though Craven's calm fluidity could only come from one who had risked his life hundreds of times in similar exchanges, for he took it all in his stride.

Sunshine glistened off of the two blades as they clashed back and forth for as long as Craven wanted to keep up the exchange. His opponent was a middling swordsman at best. Finally, Craven grew tired of the unimaginative exchanges and stepped out from one thrust and drew his blade lightly across the man's cheek, opening an inch long but very shallow cut. He was deliberately reserved in the blow so as to claim victory without doing any serious harm, but his opponent touched the wound and looked at his own blood in disgust. He then cried out angrily as he charged at Craven swinging wildly. But Craven did not back away this time. He was done playing games and instead moved forward into his opponent's attack, much to the man's surprise. He parried very close to the hilt, and his left arm quickly locked over the man's sword. He held it firm before he pressed his sword to the man's throat.

"You fools are all the same. You speak of honour, but you have none. You gave your word, and it meant nothing," snarled Craven.

The man tried to resist, but he was physically locked in place for the vice-like strength of Craven, for whom fighting was as natural as breathing.

"I owe you nothing," seethed the officer.

Craven applied more pressure to the man's sword arm. He

groaned in pain as he released his sword, and it fell to the ground. Craven rather unceremoniously kicked it across the ground, which not only showed a great lack of respect, but inevitably would damage the fine gilding on the hilt. He released his grip and pointed his sword to the man's face beside the wound he had caused.

"First blood is mine. Do not make me take a second," warned Craven.

The man knew he was done despite being furious. He walked away and collected up his sword without another word, but as he and his associates began their descent from the vantage point, another small party passed them. Four light dragoons, the officer of which had his sword slung so low the scabbard chape dragged across the ground in an intentional fashion choice. It was accompanied with an arrogant swagger the likes of which the cavalry were so fond of, for they loved to lord their status and fashion over all others. They mocked the man who had failed against Craven before approaching the Captain themselves. The officer amongst them stopped five yards short of Craven who still had his naked blade in hand.

"I suppose you come looking for me also?"

"I will not have a rogue such as you representing England here. For you are a disgrace," declared the officer.

"Come on, then," replied Craven casually.

Ferreira took a seat on a large rock, not taking the situation seriously at all, whilst Paget could not help being concerned. For no matter how good a swordsman one was, they took a risk every time they crossed blades with another, no matter their skill level. The cavalry officer drew out his sabre, a magnificent blue and gilt blade of gleaming steel. Even from a distance Paget could see the elongated and facetted pommel, which was a rarely seen, lavish and expensive option of which was both highly fashionable but also extremely effective in allowing a pistol grip style of use. Although the officer seemed to have all the money to purchase such a custom sword without knowing what its purpose was. The man's trousers were skin-tight and his curled moustache perfect. He fell into guard-like a statue, but Craven remained upright and calm, barely lifting his blade to oppose the sabre as though he was growing tired of fighting.

The officer rushed forward and swung powerful but precise blows as if to try and cut limbs clean off. Craven cut them aside before taking the fifth on a strong hanging guard, before stepping closer and smashing his elbow into the officer's face. It caused blood to flow out over his now misshapen moustache. Craven ripped the sabre from the man's grasp, and in one launched it over the ledge into the city below.

The forlorn officer looked almost ready to cry, not knowing what to do or say. He cupped his nose as blood dripped all over his bright white shirt. He was stunned. It was almost comical how easily Craven had defeated three men in one day with seemingly little effort, and that only made angry men angrier still, but he had no care for their opinions.

"Tell the next man who comes looking not to bother. I grow tired of this," snarled Craven whose head was starting to throb as the afternoon sun and his hangover began to take its toll.

CHAPTER 6

Craven sipped on some wine as he sat in the bar which had become his home, surrounded by his own soldiers. He looked restless.

"You could have killed those men very easily, or just as easily have done them harm," said Paget as he sat across the table from Craven, who did not reply.

"Why, Sir? Why when men come to kill you and mean you harm, do you not strike back with any vigour?"

"Because they are fools who do not know what they are fighting for or why?"

"You describe half the army, maybe all of it!" Moxy joked as he sat down with them in good spirits.

Craven groaned as he knew he must now give a more informed answer.

"I want to get back to the war, and wounding English officers will delay that."

"And that is the only reason?" Paget asked. He looked to Matthys, wondering if the Captain was making some efforts to heal deep wounds.

Craven said nothing as he continued to drink.

"The Captain speaks the truth. We all want back in the fight, don't we?" Moxy asked.

"But there is no war to fight, not now, not whilst we are in this stalemate at the border," replied Paget.

"And not whilst we are on leave, here to enjoy ourselves, but there is only so much rest time a fighter can have before going crazy, isn't that right?" Moxy added.

Craven nodded as there was a lot of truth to his wisdom.

"But Matthys, he won't let us go anywhere near the front lines, will he?"

Craven groaned.

"Matthys does not decide where we go or when," he muttered.

"He was right, though, wasn't he, Sir? To insist that we left the front lines. We should never have gone back there, and the Sergeant knew it, which is why he fought so hard ensure we came back here."

Craven was astonished by his courage to say it and risk his wrath, and for that reason alone he did not lash out in return, but that encouraged Paget to go on.

"We fought too hard for too long, and Matthys knew it. We all have to sit down and relax sometimes," he mused.

"Do you know what sitting around makes me feel?"

"No, Sir?"

"Tired, exhausted in fact," admitted Craven.

Paget had no answers as once again he found himself

trapped between Craven and Matthys, understanding both their points of view and being unable to find a way to console the two. The drink and food were abundant, and the Salfords gorged themselves for hours on end. They made merry as chatter and laughter filled the room, and all of their troubles seemed to fade away, at least for a while. Even Craven and Matthys were enjoying themselves, if not in the same company. Hunt entered the bar with a great if mischievous smile on his face. He rushed to Craven's side, and the Captain could see he needed to get something off his chest.

"What is it?"

"Just a little wager I have lined up which I think you might enjoy," he smirked.

"Tell me more?" Craven asked curiously, who was eager for a little adventure.

"There is a man, an officer, a true giant of a man, a pugilist, and he says he can beat any man in this army or any other."

Craven's intrigue positively exploded as he could already feel the challenge calling to him.

"And this man, he is in Lisbon?"

"He is down at the waterfront now, taking on all challengers. I hear none have fared so well thus far."

Craven smashed his cup down and shot up enthusiastically, knowing he must rise to the challenge immediately.

"Sir, perhaps this is not the best idea?" Paget asked.

"Nonsense, what is a little bit of harmless fun?"

"Perhaps fighting is best done sober?"

Craven laughed.

"There is no best time to fight, for it is any time one is

awake!"

He stormed out of the bar, though only a few had noticed him leave. Paget did not have time to attract the attention of any others as they quickly left, and he knew they must all keep a watchful eye out for one another in what was an increasingly hostile city. He and Hunt went on with Craven, but Paget was relieved to hear Ferreira's voice beside him, for the Portuguese Captain had been catching a breath of air outside in the street.

"What has him all riled up this time?" Ferreira joined Paget as they rushed on after Craven.

"The Captain goes to fight some pugilistic champion."

"Of course, he does," Ferreira sighed in frustration.

Lanterns dimly lit the streets, and so few passers-by recognised Craven as drunken soldiers staggered about the streets. They soon reached the waterfront where they could hear cheers and clapping as each good blow was celebrated. A crowd of two hundred soldiers had gathered to watch the bloody displays, both officers and common soldiers alike. Craven held up his arms and smiled as they approached.

"Now this! This is what I call entertainment!"

He pushed his way through the crowd in time to see a giant of a man smash his fist into another before bombarding him with several more blows until his opponent collapsed to the ground and gave up. Cheers rang out twice as loudly as before as they celebrated the giant's victory. An officer leapt into the ring and held his hand aloft as the victor, though he struggled to raise it completely for the height disparity between the two. The huge fighter was a head taller or more than anyone else in the crowd. He was stripped to the waist and dripping with sweat but had barely received much punishment himself. He had a light graze on one cheek and a tiny trickle of blood at the mouth, but he hardly looked as though he had received much of a challenge. The de facto announcer cried out as he sought out another challenger.

"Who else will take on the mighty Captain Edward 'The Giant' Gibbs?"

The huge fighter must be one of the biggest men in the army, for he was at least six foot five and extremely robustly built.

"He will!" Hunt roared without hesitation as he pointed to Craven, who could not refuse. He stepped forward and stripped off his clothing and handed it to Paget, just as he had as challengers came at him throughout the day. He pushed his way forward into the opening of the makeshift arena as whispers began to spread all around him. Some of them recognised Craven, and word of his name began to spread.

"Captain Craven?" asked the announcer.

"That's right."

He began to laugh as there were clearly many amongst the crowd who would enjoy seeing him get a good beating.

"We have a new challenger! Captain James Craven!"

The crowd went wild. For he still had many who admired him and now as many who considered him an adversary, or at least an undesirable. Gibbs seemed to relish the idea also.

"They say you are one of the best fighters in all of England," he said to Craven.

"That is what they say," he replied calmly.

"I should like to put that to the test," smirked Gibbs.

Craven smiled in response.

"They say you are a great fighter with a sword in hand but

let us see what kind of man you really are."

He was rather well spoken for such a hulking man as the announcer came between them.

"No gouging or biting, do you understand?"

"Yes," they both replied.

It was a simple set of rules, and there was no equipment involved. It was a good old bare knuckle boxing match as had become so popular throughout the previous century. A blood sport which was enjoyed up and down the British Isles by people of every status. The crowd was silent now as they watched with anticipation, many wanting Craven to get smashed to pieces.

Gibbs pushed out his giant limbs as he pawed at Craven, blocking his vision and threatening blows, but Craven was not intimidated. For he was known as a swordsman, but like most gladiators who fought up and down the land, he was well accustomed to fighting in every way that was practiced. He ducked under Gibbs' pawing left hand and drove an ascending straight into the giant's jaw. The blow snapped his head back, but the surprise hit just as hard as the blow. There was an audible crack upon impact. It had clearly hurt the huge man who had been expecting to toy with his smaller opponent.

Paget cheered in support, but few others did, as they wanted the big man to win. Craven was starting to understand just how widespread and successful Timmerman's campaign to smear his name had been. He had often experienced what it was like to be an unknown nobody, but he had rarely felt so hated before, but that wasn't going to make him lose the fight. If anything, it spurred him on to ensure he won it and throw it in the faces of those who despised him.

"Hit him!" Hunt cried out.

The giant came back at him but looking much more cautious now. He was very strong, that much was certain, but Craven could tell his pugilistic skills were only rudimentary. He was the sort of man who had gotten far based on his sheer strength and size, and all the physical and mental advantages it had given him over his previous opponents. But he had clearly never endured a truly hard fight against a competent opponent. Craven, on the other hand, was a good all-rounder. He was of a good height and strong body, but also highly skilled and swift in every motion.

The giant swung several punches but struggled to land any of them. Finally, he slammed a blow into Craven's flank which hurt him, and it was a reminder to get out of danger. He ducked under and away, but the giant followed him. He tried to smother him as if the body blow had spurred him on to be the savage he was born to be. But as he rushed forward, Craven rose up with an almighty uppercut which cast Gibbs' head high into the air, and he began to fall backwards. Craven followed him and dealt a crushing left hook that sent him crashing to the ground.

The crowd cheered as many had forgotten all sins and now focused on enjoying a hugely entertaining display. Craven backed away and cast his hands up in victory, not attacking the man on the ground, which was one of the few rules of such contests, including not striking below the waist. Gibbs got to one knee and had to put out one hand to support his great weight as he tried to find his balance. He tried to get back to his feet but had no balance and stumbled a few paces, crashing headfirst into the ground. He turned over and slumped out, gasping as he accepted defeat.

A few cheers rang out, but many looked upon Craven with

murderous intent, as if furious to see him victorious. He then made it all the worse by celebrating so brashly as he threw his arms about and beat his chest. Paget rushed into the arena to pass him his clothes and sword, as if to either ensure he was armed quickly in the event of an attack, or to be on their way as quickly as they could.

"A pleasure, gentlemen!" Craven roared as Paget pulled him away. He threw on his shirt and jacket and carried his sword belt. He looked bedraggled but not having a single bruise or flow of blood to show for his contest.

"You didn't have to make it look so easy," insisted Paget as they got out of earshot of the stunned crowd.

"Oh, give it up, Mr Paget and let me enjoy my moment!"

But as they left, Paget looked back to see the audience were gathering almost like an angry mob, and he pushed Craven on to get back to the security of their comrades as quickly as possible.

"What a show!" Hunt roared as he laughed all the way back to the bar.

But Paget looked at him with seething anger, knowing he was stoking the flames further. Craven didn't even see it, or perhaps he did not care. They stormed back into the bar to draw all eyes and ears.

"Captain Craven just slayed a giant!" Hunt shouted at them.

They all cheered in celebration without even knowing what he referred to, but word soon spread as the drink flowed once more. But Paget watched them in a sober state, wondering what it would all come to, as they seemed out of control, and nobody wanted to hear it.

The partying went on for hours when finally, Paget retreated to his room and watched the streets from the balcony as if expecting some trouble to come their way. He watched diligently for thirty minutes, but he soon grew tired, for he was exhausted as the whole situation was so taxing, which he almost found amusing. They had come back to Lisbon to rest and recuperate, and yet they were more on edge than ever. He finally gave up his watch, content that nothing more would come of the night, and that he was too tired to even notice it if it did for his eyes were drooping.

There was a gentle knock on his door, the very opposite of the ear-splitting experience Craven had encountered earlier that day. Though he moved to the door just as suspiciously as Craven had, with pistol in hand all the same. He prised it open slightly to be relieved that it was Charlie. He let her in before locking up and slumping into bed with half his clothes still on. The weight of the world rested on his mind, which suddenly caused a surge of energy that opened his eyes as she lay down beside him. She looked as tired as he was, but for different reasons. She reeked of wine.

"The Captain plays with fire," he said.

"Of course, he does, hasn't he always?"

"I fear this time he may not be able to fight his way out of it, and worst of all the cause of it is not his fault. Craven has made matters worse, but it is Timmerman who is to blame, and Timmerman who has turned so many officers against us. Where were they when the French came marching at our lines, beating their drums, and coming to spill our blood?" he demanded passionately.

But she groaned half-heartedly in agreement as she

cuddled into him now already half asleep.

He groaned in frustration. He wanted to talk about it further, but with Charlie asleep, his energy levels soon collapsed once more, and he fell into a deep sleep himself. But his dreams were pained, and he became intoxicated by a strangling and burning sensation of all his senses. He suddenly awoke to see wisps of smoke flooding in through the door frame. He coughed as he got up and instantly realised the sensations were not just in his dreams but were real. He shook Charlie.

"Get up, get up!"

She began to rise as he rushed to the balcony to check the scene around them. In the alley below he could make out several British officers with torches in hand. One of them was the man who Craven had disarmed and forced him to leave his sword in the very same street. More smoke was arising from the floors below, and Paget leant down to see the lick of flames from the windows on the lowest floor where the bar had been set alight. There was no uncertainty as to who had started it and why, and yet he was aghast that they would take such a drastic measure. He looked horrified, for he imagined any of the officers who would come for them would attack them with swords and fists, and not in such a barbaric manner.

"Fire!" Paget shouted at the top of his voice.

He cried out again as he banged loudly on the wall beside him. He kept crying out and watched as the officers in the street turned and walked away, leaving them without any remorse to die in the most dreadful of ways, and murdering dozens of the Salfords who were boarding there, as well as the bar owners. Paget rushed back to Charlie who was starting to realise what was happening as he ripped the door open. Smoke flooded into the room. He grabbed his jacket and placed it to his mouth before grabbing his weapons, not just to use for defence if they escaped but because they were the most valuable physical things he had in the country.

"Come on!" Charlie yelled. She was already ahead of him.

They reached the corridor to find flames licking up the wooden walls. She pulled him one way, but he resisted and instead led her back to Craven's room. He beat heavily on the door with the butt of his pistol but could get no response, and so he tried to smash through it with his body but bounced off for he had so little mass.

"Move aside!"

Birback charged like a raging bull and flew into the door, knocking it from its hinges. It landed on the floor beside Craven's bed with such a crash as to finally wake him up.

"Come on, Sir, we have to go before the whole building comes down around us!" Paget yelled as he gathered up the Captain's things.

They rushed on, the floorboards creaking as they began to give way, as everyone inside rushed towards the stairs to find flames lashing out towards them. They turned and fled for the only other way out, a very narrow stairway used by staff, but to their relief it was flooded with smoke and not flames. They rushed out and down to the lower floor where Craven stopped for a moment to see the bar in flames and all the drink behind it consumed by the fire. It was a tragic sight.

"Come on, Sir!" Paget yelled in frustration.

They ran on through the smoke and flames and burst out onto the street. They finally came to a halt at a safe distance away just as teams arrived with buckets to try and fight the fire, but there would be no saving the bar. They could only try to contain the fire and stop it spreading across the city. The bar owners had made it out alive but looked in despair as all they had went up in flames.

"Is everyone here?" Matthys cried out as he checked their numbers.

Many coughed and spluttered, as some put out the flames of their clothing and wiped their soot covered faces. Craven seemed to have gotten out of it unscathed, and yet he looked furious.

"This was Timmerman's doing and the lies he has spread!"

"We don't know that," Matthys insisted as he tried to calm the situation.

"Yes, we do. I saw them, men with torches in the street," admitted Paget.

"And you recognised them?" Matthys asked.

"I did."

"Well?"

"Some of them were the same men who came looking to kill you, Sir."

Craven was shaking with rage, imagining what he would do to them as he watched the bar be engulfed in flames, the same bar which had become a home to them all and had been full of so many found memories. Yet Matthys watched in despair as he imagined the response which might follow.

CHAPTER 7

Craven moved through the smoking ashes of the former bar as he and the others looked for anything they could retrieve. Many had left weapons, uniform items, and personal effects and fled for their lives. The owners, a husband and wife broke down in tears in the street, having lost everything. It was a disaster, and there was no other word for it. Many of them coughed violently from the smoke they had inhaled. Paget knelt down in the ruins and pulled out a long object which was badly scorched. He knocked black soot aside, and Craven recognised it as the hunting rifle the Lieutenant's father had given him, a piece he was very fond of. He had shown much skill with it, striking many a Frenchman with it in a way any rifleman would be proud of and Craven himself could only dream of. The Captain felt disgusted and almost physically sick of the sight as he saw the sorrow in Paget's eyes, as if he had lost a close friend.

Several of the others had similar experiences if not so

devastating as they pulled their own possessions from the ruins, whilst many uniform items had been lost and they knew would be hard to replace. They were at least fortunate they did not have an authority to answer to for losing the King's equipment, as Craven had maintained a lax discipline throughout.

"You might have beaten those men in contests, but they had the last laugh, didn't they, Sir? For they burnt our world down," said Paget.

Craven could find no words as he felt the anger flow through his body as his blood began to boil.

"Bastards must pay," growled Birback.

Craven tried to speak but coughed further before finally being able to get a few words out.

"We will find whoever did this, and they will pay," he growled in a gruff and coarse voice even worse than from his hangover the day before.

"You won't have to look far," replied Hunt.

Craven looked stunned as he followed Hunt's gaze to the street ahead where several dozen soldiers approached as a rabble, and yet there were many junior officers amongst them. They came with swords in hand, whilst others carried anything they could use as a percussive tool from table legs and planks, to walking canes, and even rammers and sponge rods from artillery pieces. They came to do battle as if it were some medieval brawl where they smashed each other's brains with crude blunt and sharp implements alike. Birback was grinning like a fool as if it was the most beautiful thing he had ever seen, imagining himself wading into the mob and fighting like a fanatic.

"Arm yourselves!" Craven ordered.

Those who had swords drew them whilst others picked up rubble, rocks, broken furniture, broken bottles, and anything else they could find that would do harm as they stepped out from the rubble. The two sides came head to head, stopping just ten yards from one another in the calm before the storm.

Craven already had his sword in hand, but he drew out his dirk as well, ready to cause as much carnage as he could without any care for the lives of those before them, even if they did wear British uniforms. He hated them even more than many of the French they had opposed on the battlefield, for these men were their sworn brothers. It was a betrayal in his eyes, and that admonished him of all the sins he was about to commit. He wanted blood at any cost, and he could not think of anything else. Nobody said a word, for there was nothing which could change the minds of any soldier on either side. They hated one another as if they had been born to such a long-lasting feud which few could even explain anymore, but all knew as a fact.

There was near silence as the two groups glared at one another with murderous intent. The only sound which emanated through the streets was the weeping of the bar owners who had lost more than any of them, for it had cost no lives, but a lifetime's livelihood.

"Come on!" Craven shouted angrily.

But the gallop of horses' hooves broke the silence after his cry. Nobody moved as a single rider galloped onto the scene. He pushed through the lines to take up position between the two sides who were almost frothing at the mouth, as they prepared to do battle to the death if need be. It was Major Spring, who was alone and did not even have a weapon in hand. His sword was still sheathed and hanging from his sword belt. He wheeled about his horse, using it to create a barrier between the two opposing forces before finally coming to a standstill. He was breathing hard as if having travelled far and with great urgency, and his horse was showing the same signs. He looked just as angry as Craven.

"This is over. You will disperse, and that is an order from Wellington himself!"

Craven looked angry, but the other side seemed to not even take notice as if assuming the orders related to Craven and his Salfords.

"Don't do this," he pleaded with Craven.

"These men came here to kill us all. They meant to burn us all to the ground!"

"But they did not, and more bloodshed will do no good."

There was no reply, but Spring noticed the other side approach a few steps, and he turned his horse about to face them in disbelief and disgust.

"What do you idiots think you are doing?"

"Craven is a disgrace and brings dishonour to us all!" cried the officer who had lost his sword to Craven in the same street.

"A disgrace?" Spring asked in disbelief, "Listen to me now and hear me, for I speak with the authority of Lord Wellington. This man you come here to kill, Captain Craven and his Salfords, they have done more in this war than you will ever do or could even dream of achieving. If you do not believe me, then you can answer to Wellington himself because we have both seen the evidence of such with our own eyes. Turn away and never return, or I will ensure you all go before a court martial and never serve in this army ever again!"

Those who had come looking for a fight had done so with

such confidence and conviction, but they wavered now upon the words of the Major, who drew his sword to drive his point home.

"Leave, or I will personally deal with any man who stays!"

The mob soon fragmented as they lost heart and dared not oppose one of Wellington's staff, but Spring turned back to see Craven's comrades would not be so easily stood down. They were a hundred times more angry and ready to spill blood than those who had come to start the fight.

"End this now, promise me," he pleaded.

"Why would we? Those bastards tried to burn us alive and spit on us, and for what? Because we stood up for an honourable man?" Craven protested.

"Because I am asking you to. Because this madness must come to an end. This chaos could have spread, and half the city could have burnt to the ground because of this feud."

"Not because of our actions," snapped Craven.

"No, but I cannot change what happened. I can only try and save this situation before it turns to utter chaos." Spring looked out to the rest of the Salfords and addressed them directly with a booming voice.

"Remember the Lines of Torres Vedras. Remember what cost was paid to save this city. Remember the blood which was spilled and the sacrifices which were made. You do not deserve this violence, but neither does Lisbon. Think of the city and remember its people!"

Many of them looked to Ferreira for his opinion, it being his home city, but the Portuguese Captain looked to Craven, trusting in him to make the right decision.

"What would you do?" Craven asked him, feeling a little

guilty for the chaos he had caused.

"To hell with them," snapped Hunt.

But nobody listened to him as they focused on those who mattered most.

Ferreira looked deeply uncomfortable, for he sympathised with Craven's case, but he was sick of the fighting between allies and saddened to see a well-known landmark of his home city be burned to the ground.

"This has to end. We live to fight another day," he admitted.

Craven exited his stable fighting position and stood upright, taking a deep breath as he calmed himself. He sheathed his sword and dirk.

"This is wrong, all of it, and you know it," he said to Major Spring.

"Yes, it is," admitted Spring.

"But we will see an end to it. We will not seek vengeance tonight but know that anyone who means to do me and my own harm will not be tolerated."

Spring sighed, knowing Craven would hold him to that whether he agreed to it or not.

"There is a war to fight, Craven, and we will not win it fighting amongst ourselves."

His words cut deep as Craven knew it was true.

"What would you have us do? That bastard Timmerman has turned half the damned city against us, and they want our blood? Not Frenchmen, but redcoats."

Spring sighed with frustration.

"Gather all your men and meet me at the place where you felled the giant Gibbs in two hours."

"You saw that?" smiled Craven.

"No, but I know what happened and where, for that is my job, to know all that goes on."

Craven nodded in appreciation for his work.

"And Timmerman, what will you do about him?"

"For what? Spreading word about the things that you did?" Spring replied coarsely.

"Colonel Bevan was no coward, and I will not hear otherwise!"

"From what I understand you might be right, but that is not my decision to make. If you want to redeem Bevan and yourself, you must find a way, for I cannot."

Craven sighed in frustration as it was merely a distraction from what mattered, but Spring did not want to hear it, who was still alone, there being no sign of any escorts. He had taken a great risk getting in between two violent gangs of soldiers who wanted one another's blood, and that garnered him a lot of respect with Craven.

"Don't be late, Captain. Life must go on and the war must go on. I have many duties to attend to, and if I cannot resolve this soon, I will be forced to take measures which you will not appreciate."

"And the alternative?"

"You do what you are ordered to do by Wellington himself."

Craven shrugged in agreement.

"Don't make this worse than it is, Craven. It is dirty business, but you chose to make it this way. Don't throw everything away over a dead man."

Spring left without another word being unwilling to argue

further and showing no flexibility at all, as he expected his orders to be followed, which felt more like demands to Craven who was still seething.

"Are you going to let this stand?" Hunt tried to rile Craven up once more, imagining the devastation he might bring if he swept through the city like a wild banshee. Craven was close to falling into such a craze as he could barely contain himself.

"Enough of this, it can't go on. We can't keep fighting amongst ourselves," pleaded Paget.

Matthys was relieved to hear him say it. He desperately wanted to be the voice of reason himself, but he knew it would anger Craven further to hear it from his mouth.

Craven turned angrily toward Paget but found his rage reduced as he looked upon the forlorn young officer with his ruined rifle. The Lieutenant had not even tried to arm himself during the standoff with the mob who had burnt down the bar with them inside and come to finish the job. He had no stomach for it, and yet Archie Hunt continued to press for the violence to continue to escalate.

"They tried to burn us all alive! Will you let this stand?"

Birback groaned in agreement.

"If you pursue this fight any further, I cannot follow you, and I will not. I will resign my commission if you take this path," declared Paget.

Charlie could barely believe what she was hearing. She was almost as eager for blood as Birback, but Paget's words were enough to pause and make her think about how much it was affecting them all.

Amyn who had been silent throughout came forward to speak, for nobody else would as the group seemed to be fracturing into those who wanted to wreak havoc across Lisbon and those who wanted the complete opposite.

"Hear me," he declared with his sword still in hand, having expected a fight and being fully ready and prepared for it, "My people met their end because they were too few and too weak. Whatever you think of those who did this to us, if we keep killing one another, then you will give victory to Napoleon. This violence will never come to an end whilst both sides pursue it relentlessly."

"It is not us who looked for this," snapped Craven defensively.

"Maybe not, but you have done nothing to discourage it. You have looked for fights, and you have humiliated men and given them no choice but to strike back at you."

Craven sighed in frustration as he knew it was true, but he felt justified in much of it.

"Those men did not need to come and look for me. They came to try and kill me, what would you have me do?"

"Snub them. Deny them a contest with blades, for no good can come of it."

Craven tutted as if that was an impossibility.

"Would it be so hard to not fight?"

Craven wanted to say yes, and he thought it, but he looked back to Paget and the anguish in his eyes. He couldn't understand how he had somehow become the villain in all of this, but he knew something had to change.

"What do we do?" he asked, finally accepting he did not have the answers and could not decide for them all. He posed his question to Paget, genuinely asking him for advice on how to lead them all.

"Let us go and do as Major Spring ordered and see where it takes us, Sir. We have achieved so much in this war, but there is so much more to do, and it will not be accomplished by fighting our own soldiers here in Lisbon."

"And Bevan? You would have me let his honour be dragged through the dirt?"

"I am afraid that damage is already done. I hate it, I hate even saying it, but it is the truth. All we can do now is not get dragged through the same mud with the poor Colonel," admitted Paget.

"Then we abandon him and his name?"

"If that is what we must do. This is war, Captain, and you have told me many times that a man must do what is necessary to win. Sometimes that means doing things which one would never dream of. I wish this was a perfect world. I wish for many things. I wish this damned war had not cost so many lives, but some things are beyond our control. Let this go and let us all get on with our lives, without having to look over our shoulders everywhere we go for fear of being stabbed in the back, not by some French spy, but by our own soldiers."

Craven sighed as he rubbed his face with exhaustion before looking around at all who awaited his orders. Even those like Birback who were wanting to fight looked exhausted. Only Hunt seemed to have any fire left in him.

"Is this what you want of me? Do you agree with the Lieutenant?"

"I do," declared Charlie.

She did not fully agree with his sentiments, but she would back him anyway.

Hawkshaw looked indifferent to it all, either through not

knowing how to think, or perhaps still suffering from the brain fog of his concussion. Craven looked around at the faces of those who had fought by his side through the long war in Portugal and Spain, and he finally reached Matthys. Neither of them said a word. There was still a lot of animosity between the two, and yet Craven knew his opinion was worth far more than most, for he was always clear-headed.

"Gather up the men, be on your watch for trouble but do not look for it. We will do as Major Spring asks of us."

Paget looked relieved, more than any of them. The rest of the regiment soon gathered, making them a force to be reckoned with, but Craven sat idle until it was time to go to meet Spring. He led them on, wandering with a vagueness and lack of determination that few of them had ever seen from him.

"What will become of us, Sir?" Paget asked as he walked beside Craven.

"Your guess is as good as mine."

They gathered at the spot as had been ordered and formed up ready for the Major. They looked a ragged bunch, almost all of them missing some items of clothing or weapons. They looked almost like a poorly equipped militia. Craven had saved his tunic and weapons but was missing his officers sash and shako. Somehow, Ferreira had managed to keep onto all of his equipment and looked in remarkably smart condition compared to most. It was not long before Major Spring approached, and he had Thornhill with him, as well as thirty of the town's militia in case of any unrest. They stopped well short of the Salfords as the two British officers approached.

"You have been quite the headache for us all," insisted Thornhill.

"Good," smirked Craven before Spring went on.

"Listen, Captain, the situation here is grave. This level of unrest is damaging to us all, not just for the parties involved, but for this city and for the reputation of the entire army. How do you think the people of Lisbon will feel towards our army when this sort of senseless violence goes on? What will Napoleon think when he hears our officers are killing one another at will?"

"I should imagine he would understand, for the French love to duel, they embrace it at every turn."

But Spring sighed in frustration, having hoped for a more understanding response. Seeing how casual the address had been, the rest of the officers of the Salfords closed in around them to hear their fate to be revealed for themselves.

"What are our orders?" Ferreira asked.

Spring sighed as he knew they would not like what was about to come next.

"Come on, Major, let us hear it," insisted Craven.

"We need you out of here."

"That can be arranged."

"Not out of this city, out of this country. We are sending you back to England," added Major Spring.

"England, but the war is here," protested Craven.

"The war is here in Lisbon at present, and that must stop. You have made many enemies, Captain."

Craven sighed angrily.

"Come on, Captain, you have been here for a few years now, and the war is not changing soon, we are at a standstill. Go home, get some rest, recruit some new blood for the Salfords, and get away from all of this madness," added Thornhill as he tried to smooth over the whole affair.

Craven was deep in thought, but as he looked back to the two Majors, he could see they were in no mood to argue.

"I don't have a choice, do I?"

"These are your orders directly from Wellington himself. You have done great things in this war, Captain, but the best thing for all of us now is to get you clear of this place, at least for a while. Go home, spend a few months in England, heal those wounds, gather new strength, and come back better than ever," replied Spring.

"You think time will change any of this?"

"Of course, it will. The squabbles of men soon get forgotten in time when they have many more things to worry about. If you stay here, the city will descend into chaos, but with a little time we can move past all of this."

"And the Portuguese troops who serve with us?"

"They can return home or stay here in Lisbon. I will ensure they continue to receive pay," replied Spring.

"I want to stay, Sir," insisted Hawkshaw.

Thornhill could hardly believe what he was hearing as he looked back in utter contempt.

"You? You are the reason all of this began. You who should have returned to England but instead got into bed with Timmerman's wife. Only a fool could not know the perils that would unleash. No, Captain, you will not stay in Lisbon, for you are the worst of the bunch. You will gather up your things and depart for England today. And you will not look back, and you will not continue this madness back in England. Remember this, all of you. Here in the Iberian Peninsula you have been allowed to get away with almost anything, bloody murder I would say, but the authorities in England won't be so lenient. You are officers and gentlemen, and you will be expected to act like them," demanded Spring.

"Like the gentlemen who tried to burn us all alive?" Craven replied.

"You are not the innocent party here, Captain, and you would do well to remember that. You will board the Minerva this afternoon and soon be under way for Portsmouth. What you do with your time in England is down to you, but I advise you to use it wisely."

Spring pointed to the vessel moored in the harbour. She was a respectable thirty-two-gun Royal Navy frigate, far more impressive than many of the vessels they had travelled on before. Yet Craven still looked lost and almost in despair.

"This is not a punishment, Captain. These are merely your orders for which have been considered for the best of outcomes for us all. You have a chance to go home and step away from this war for a while. Enjoy it."

"I should like to go with them, Sir," insisted Ferreira.

"And I would accompany you, for I should like to see the country of which I now wear the uniform," added Gamboa.

"As you wish," replied Spring.

The two Majors waited for Craven to accept his orders, seemingly unsure how he would react, but finally he looked to Quental.

"Inform the men. Let them return to their families, but I want two days of training every week, do you understand?"

"Yes, Sir."

"Then to England we go," replied Craven.

"Safe travels," declared Spring as he and Thornhill walked away, leaving the militia in place to maintain order until they had left.

Spring shook his head in amazement as he took out a guinea coin and tossed it to Thornhill.

"I am amazed, but you were right," he said, having lost a wager that Craven would accept his fate and leave the country.

"Craven is not a stupid man, and I imagine he is quite sick of this city and the misery it has brought," replied Thornhill.

"Indeed, but Craven is built for war. God save England on his return."

They both chuckled along at the prospect of the chaos he would cause.

CHAPTER 8

"How long will you be gone?" Lady Sarmento asked as she waited at the harbour side to see them depart with an umbrella to keep the sun from her face.

"It cannot be long, for the war will soon continue and this is where we are needed," replied Craven.

She looked sad at their departure, but it was more than that as she looked quite uncomfortable.

"I am sorry I did not do more to defend you," she finally declared.

"You did what you had to do, same as the rest of us. You fight your battles just like we do." Craven had long since forgotten her unwillingness to stand up for him before her rude guests.

"Look after them, for when you have friends like that you must hold most tightly onto them," she replied as she looked at his comrades gathering their few belongings in readiness to leave.

"If Timmerman continues to harass you, be sure to go to Major Spring, for he will deal with it."

"I can handle Timmerman."

He nodded agreement as he looked out to sea, deep in thought as to what the next few weeks would bring.

"It is an honourable thing you did, to stand up for Colonel Bevan when no other man would."

"And look where it has gotten me? I have achieved nothing and only brought us pain."

"Don't be so sure. Your words carry weight and others will listen. Don't ever be sorry for standing up for what is right."

"Is that what I was doing?" Craven pondered.

"Absolutely, for you had no other reason to want to protect the Colonel's name."

"Perhaps I felt compelled, hoping that someone else would do the same for me if my name was ever dragged through the muck after I am dead."

She laughed.

"When has James Craven ever cared about his name or what it meant after death?"

He shrugged as there was some truth to it, and yet a few years of war in the Peninsula had changed him greatly, and she could see it on his face.

"Really? That has changed?"

"I didn't used to care because I had no reason to, but when you spend enough time with people you love and who love you, perhaps that changes," he replied quietly.

"Well, Captain Craven, I am stunned, for I never thought I would see the day."

"They say war changes all of us. Some say it numbs the senses and leaves one cold, but I must admit I have found quite the opposite."

"You have found a purpose."

"Yes, perhaps I have," he smiled.

"Good luck in England, Captain. Break hearts, but not heads."

"I'll do my best."

The handful of Salfords who were making the return to England boarded the Minerva without drama or incident. The sailors aboard had no knowledge or care for the disputes which had rocked Lisbon, and even if they did, they would more than likely welcome the troublemakers. For they loved nothing more than to cause absolute chaos in port cities as a drunken rabble when on shore leave.

Many of those travelling with Craven had arrived in Portugal with him, but he returned now with even more, including several men who had never seen his home country before, including Amyn who followed him. He had no reason to stay in Portugal, for his home now was with his comrades and not any physical place he could name. Paget was quick to see to the correct and careful loading of Augustus in the hold who he was always so precious and protective of. They took up positions on the deck, breathing in the fresh sea air, which would be most welcome as they got underway for what could be a week's journey, depending on the winds.

Spring and Thornhill watched beside Lady Sarmento as the roguish Captain departed the city, relieved that the chaos was finally over.

"It was a wise idea, My Lady, to send him back to England,

but I fear he will only stir up trouble somewhere new," declared Spring.

"But not under our watch at least," replied Thornhill, who was equally as relieved to be able to resume life as normal.

"You treat the Captain like a weapon and are surprised when he does damage," declared the Lady.

"That man was born to be a weapon," replied Spring.

Craven leant out over the edge of the vessel as he looked back towards Lisbon, the city which had been at the heart of the entire war since it began. It was unscathed by the recent war and was bustling like never before.

"I will miss it, this place," said Paget.

They had been in the country for so long they had forgotten all else as it had become their home. Though they would not miss the heat and welcomed a cooler few months to get some rest.

"I couldn't not stand up for Colonel Bevan. His story is a tragedy."

"Yes, it is, Sir, but there are so many tragedies, and we cannot be hung up on any of them for too long, or else we will be swallowed up by them and become one ourselves. Would you have us remembered the same way as the Colonel?"

Craven sighed as it was an awful position to be put in.

"You did not even know the Colonel, not really. Of all the soldiers we have fought beside, our time with the Colonel was insignificant. You must let it go, Sir, for all our sakes," pleaded Paget.

"You once told me that honour was everything."

"I was wrong. I had some idea of what soldiering was and I was wrong, at least in some regards."

"Does any man truly know what they are doing out here?" Craven pondered as he watched the harbour fade from view as they got underway.

The realisation that they were stepping away from the war and returning home was quickly setting in for all of them. It was a strange sensation to realise that England was only a week away, or a few days on a fast ship, and yet they had not seen their country for years. It felt like a great weight had been lifted from their shoulders.

As Craven lay down in a hammock, he dropped off into a deep sleep almost instantly, for he no longer had such heavy weights weighing on his mind nor men coming to kill him. He awoke to the morning sun lighting the cabin through an open gun port as they slept between the guns. He could hear the clash of sticks on deck and the shuffle of feet. He knew that sound so well. He leapt from his bed with a spring in his step as he rushed up on deck. Dozens of the ship's crew were practicing sword drills in lines and by command.

The sight brought a smile to his face. He almost felt reborn as he was feeling refreshed. The sea breeze blew across his face as he listened to the words of command roar and the clash of sticks echo. It was sweet music to his ears as he watched sweat drip from the faces of the sailors. They must have been at it for some time, but they were fit and well-conditioned. That had to mean they were accustomed to regular practice, as not even the fittest sailors could conduct hours of sword drill without regular and rigorous training over an extended period. Finally, the men were released from their structured line where they moved on command and began to fight with one another in one-on-one fencing contests.

"Do they meet with your approval?" The ship's Captain stepped up beside Craven.

Craven smiled.

"Yes, indeed," he replied quite casually.

The two men shared the same rank, but it signified a very different level of authority in the Royal Navy, where a Captain was as a Colonel in the army, yet Craven conversed with him quite casually, as he seemed a man who he would get on well with.

"Captain Craven," declared Craven as an introduction.

"Captain Burslem." The man was of slight but strong build, like a steel cable. He had the look of a man who had been everywhere and done everything, and yet somehow had not become an angry and cynical recluse as so many had before him. He commanded respect and authority, but not because he enforced it with the lash, but because of his calm confidence and leadership.

"You are the Craven I hear so much about, the man who would win this war by the sword."

"Many wise men have told me to do what I am best at. I am no marksman, but I can manipulate a sword as if it were my own body."

"Yes, so I hear."

"You train your men regularly with the sword?" Craven asked as he marvelled at the display.

"You know the answer to that."

He did indeed, as there was a lot of skill on display. The crew fought with skill and precision, their bodies strong and their reactions sharp.

Craven looked to a rack of cutlasses and could see they

were well cleaned and maintained, and the black japanning of the cast iron grips was well worn. A sort of thick paint which was used to preserve certain metal objects on board seafaring vessels, for the salt water was brutally abrasive all year round. Craven did not envy the work it would require to keep maintaining a sword at sea, where both moisture and salt were forever a problem.

"Do you have much use for your cutlasses?"

"Plenty."

"You still encounter such threats?" Craven was surprised, as since Nelson's defeat of the French and Spanish fleets at Trafalgar the British fleet had ruled the waves. It was the decisive victory which had kept England safe from a French invasion and underpinned the operations in the Peninsula campaign to this day.

"The Minerva has had plenty of work countering privateers about Spain and Portugal since long before I took command."

"Many captains spend little time or effort on the sword, instead relying on the guns and muskets and perhaps the raw ferocity of their crews."

"I would not rely on men's base instincts to win a battle, as if they are barbarians flailing wildly. A man must be skilled in all things necessary to prevail in any situation, would you not agree?"

Craven nodded. He liked this Captain.

"Not all respect the sword as this," he replied.

"There will come a day when swords no longer have any purpose in war, for the science of war is ever evolving, but it shall not be in our lifetimes."

Craven had never even considered the possibility as swords had been the foundation of his life. The prospect of them becoming obsolete was terrifying, for he did not know what place there would be left for him in the world.

"Don't worry, Captain, it will be far into the future," added Burslem.

"And you, Captain? Will the age of sail come to an end?"

"Most certainly, for have you not seen the marvellous steamboat creations?"

Craven shook his head.

"Science moves on, Captain. It keeps moving on and waits for no man, and one day all that we do here will seem quite the quaint and inefficient exercise," smiled Burslem.

"Thankfully we will never see it. I cannot imagine a world without a sword by my side."

"Indeed, we have far greater worries in our days now ahead, for Napoleon must be stopped."

"And yet I am going in the wrong direction for that, back to England whilst the war goes on here in Portugal."

"When I sail back to England, is this ship no longer fighting the war? No, it is just part of the workings. Just as the recruiting sergeant in the tavern and the worker in the mill, all parts of the great machine of war."

Craven looked impressed. The ship's Captain was clearly a worldly man with an interesting perspective. It was how he imagined Paget would talk in another ten to twenty years, leading a Brigade if he had not yet gone into politics, which is where he imagined the young man.

"You must be a great swordsman, for I have heard it said by some that you are the best in all of England."

"If people say it, then it must surely be true," smiled Craven.

"My crew could always do with fresh challenges; will you take on a few challengers?"

"It would be my pleasure."

Craven stripped off his sword belt and jacket. The ship's Captain called all who were training with their sticks to stop and gather around so that he could address them, and that they would create a small arena, far smaller on the deck of the ship than when he had taken on the giant Gibbs.

"Captain Craven here is a master of the sword, and his skills are becoming as famous as his eagerness to fight. Who amongst you would rise to the challenge of giving the Captain a contest with sticks and show this land lubber what a Royal Navy swordsman is made of?"

A dozen men's hands show up as they volunteered without hesitation, and the rest looked eager to see the display.

"Do you take on all comers?" Burslem asked Craven.

"Always," he smirked as Burslem took a singlestick from one of his crew and passed it to him. It was a fine quality ash stave with a hardened and well used leather basket. The sort of tool commonly seen in fencing schools and army exercises, but it surprised him to see them at sea, where so often the crews of ships trained with merely a length of wood, if at all. It showed Burslem's attention to the training of his crew as they were able to train much harder and in far more a realistic fashion with a well-constructed training tool.

"Who will be first?" Burslem asked.

A young but strongly built and eager man leapt forward to take the first shot at Craven. He saluted respectfully but quickly went to guard, desperate to put his skills to the test. Craven launched a cut for his head with only half his strength to test the man's defences. He lifted his stick into a parry before responding quickly to Craven's head. Craven then tried a thrust but found the same response. The sailor was smiling, thinking he was doing well. There was no doubt he had a solid foundation of training and good speed also, but Craven was initially putting him to the test. This time he launched a cut towards the man's head but in an almost horizontal fashion to draw his parry wide. As the man's stick moved out from his body to make the parry, he found Craven's singlestick was nowhere to be found. It had already turned over and snapped down onto the bone of his forearm just below the elbow. The blow hurt a little, but it was more the surprise which shocked the eager young man who had thought he was doing well. A cheer rang out from his comrades as they celebrated the victory despite it not being one of their own.

"Next!" Burslem roared.

The next man, having seen his comrade's defeat, started out very differently, with a flurry of blows as he tried to overwhelm Craven with a torrent of blows in the hope that one would get through. But Craven took every blow before snapping one in of his own between the blows of his attacker. It was a very fast vertical cut launched with the quick twitch of his fingers and wrist. It sent his stick down onto the crown of the man's head, which sent him staggering back.

"Next!"

He fought them one after another with even more volunteering to take their turn, thinking they had found a way through the Captain's guard, or perhaps just eager to share a fight with such a great swordsman as they were all in good spirits. It was a testament to the ship's Captain that his crew fought hard and competitively, but not in anger or with any intent to do serious harm to those they practiced against.

Craven was in his element as he fought one after another, the sea breeze keeping him cool and energetic throughout. His friends and comrades watched on with glee to see him return to top form. No longer was he fighting with anger and bitterness and the disillusionment they had seen in Lisbon; he was fighting for the love of the challenge as he eagerly asked for one fight after another. The training went on for hours until finally Burslem brought it to an end so that the men could rest a little before going about their duties. The sword practice was in itself a training exercise, and yet the crew seemed to love it almost as much as taking shore leave. As the singlesticks were stowed away, the ship's Captain approached Craven. He looked highly impressed.

"That was quite the display. I am not sure I saw one of my boys land any on you."

"They are good fighters. Fencing has been my life. I have fought for pay, I have fought on the stage and for fame, and I have fought the best. Your crew have everything they need to win a battle, and you should be proud of them, for they would roll over the French."

"Thank you, that is very kind."

"Oh, no, I do not say it out of kindness but appreciation for those who continue to respect and train the art and science of defence."

"Then I would ask you a favour, Captain."

"Yes?"

"We have the pleasure of your company for this week, and there will be no work, save for if we encounter some engagement with the French, of which is almost an impossibility on this route. My crew would benefit greatly from your insight and your skills. Would you train with a party every day? Or do I ask too much?"

"It would be my pleasure," replied Craven who was relieved to have something fun to do.

Paget looked relieved to see the Captain come out of the stupor of daily drinking without any ambition or purpose. He wondered if the burning down of the bar was the best thing that could have happened for them all. The officers, Craven, Ferreira, and Paget soon found themselves at the dining table with the ship's senior officers for an evening meal. They were all in good spirits, and there was none of the animosity so often felt between army and navy officers. Burslem welcomed them as honoured guests, yet none of his officers could get a word in as he bombarded Craven with questions. Always looking to learn and know more.

"I hear you have fought at sea," said Burslem.

Craven was surprised to hear anyone was familiar with his modest naval adventures.

"Word spreads quickly whenever you sail into port."

"Yes, nothing like the great battles of Nelson, but a few small encounters."

"Boarding actions, yes?"

Craven nodded as he sipped on some wine, knowing it would not flow in such huge quantities as in Lisbon, and also not wanting to appear as a drunkard before the respectable Burslem.

"And you won a boarding action whilst outnumbered? That is quite a feat."

"Skills, tricks, and training."

"All of those things and more, for I imagine your tenacity must answer in some part for the success."

Craven shrugged modestly.

"The Captain is too modest, for I have seen him run into the chaos of battle against odds one could never imagine overcoming," added Paget.

"And you have not?" smiled Craven, remembering the times Paget had rushed into battle without any concern in the world.

The group fell silent as a question weighed heavily on Burslem, and he soon came out with it.

"Tell me, Captain, are we winning this war?"

"Yes, and no," admitted Craven.

"Go on."

"We win many battles. Wellington is a great tactician, but he cannot achieve the impossible. We are forever under supplied and lacking in troops, whilst the French always have more. Always more no matter how many we shoot down."

Burslem looked troubled by the prospect but also appreciated the honest assessment. He soon moved the conversation on to lighter topics as they made the best of the evening. It was a strange experience for Craven who was not accustomed to wining and dining with the officers, having always spent his time with his closest friends despite the difference in their rank and status. He did not see the divide between officers and enlisted soldiers. He had long been accustomed to being a leader since his gladiatorial days but didn't much care for the rigidly enforced division between the officer elite. And yet in the ship's officers he found a more down to earth and level-headed set of officers who were as much a breath of fresh air as the sea breeze.

The evening went well with polite conversation and good banter alike, but Craven was soon awaking again in his hammock, once again feeling refreshed. The two hours of sword training the day before had ensured he did not struggle to get off to sleep. It was not long before the morning training commenced again, as a new group of sailors took their turns at testing themselves against Craven with more bouts continuing all around them. The ship's deck was alive with activity.

Matthys watched Craven with some hope that he was returning to the man he had become. The man who had been forged in battle in Portugal and Spain, and not the one who had drunken himself into oblivion whilst seeking out trouble in Lisbon. Yet as one fight finished, he noticed Craven go to Hunt, who was keeping tally in a small book. Craven went back to fight but then sat out for a few moments, chatting further with Hunt as he made notes.

"A fine sight, is it not?" Paget asked as he stepped up beside the Sergeant.

"Yes, quite."

But doubts flooded his mind once again, as he could see Hunt dragging Craven back into the grim depths of gambling, for which he had always despised and seen so many men be swallowed up whole by. Yet he could not know for certain that is what he was seeing and so said nothing, hoping and praying he was wrong.

"A fine display indeed," he muttered.

CHAPTER 9

"There she is, Sir, England!" Paget cried excitedly.

Craven was stunned by the sight, almost as if he had never expected to see the shores of his home country ever again. He was not much of a patriotic man, but the calling of home was undeniable. They sailed into the great naval depot at Portsmouth, the home of the Royal Navy, the most powerful fleet in the world since Nelson's great victory at Trafalgar. And there in the port they could see the magnificent ship which served as Nelson's flagship on that fateful day, HMS Victory. The battle was a triumph which had cost the Admiral his life but saved England from invasion. For the battle of Trafalgar would forever be remembered as one of the greatest and most decisive military victories in history, a bitter wound for Napoleon which would never heal, and one he was constantly reminded of. Burslem's frigate was a modest warship beside the mighty HMS Victory as they sailed fairly close to the iconic vessel. It had been anchored in full view of all who came and went through the port as though she was a guardian of the nation.

Paget marvelled at the great vessel, awestruck. She was already a very old vessel when Nelson had led her into battle at Trafalgar in 1805, having been launched in 1765 and first commissioned in 1778. She'd had a hard service life, and the brutal battle of Trafalgar had done tremendous damage to the vessel, for which no amount of repairs could ever entirely heal.

"Incredible, is she not, Sir?"

He shrugged, for Victory was a large ship but he didn't have much care for the sea.

"Is she not an inspiration, Sir? Hope for us all," added Paget.

"How so?" Craven asked curiously.

"By all accounts the HMS Victory should have left the service many years ago, long before Trafalgar. She was an old ship, riddled with defects and laid up as a hospital ship before Napoleon ever even rose to power. It was through a freak accident and the loss of the Impregnable that the Royal Navy found itself short of a three-deck ship of the line. You see the Victory was recommissioned and saved from a miserable existence to fade away never having achieved anything of note. And yet she went on to become the great hero we know today. She is an inspiration, Sir, to us all. For if that old wreck of a vessel can rise to become the bane of Napoleon, so can we all," declared Paget proudly.

Craven suddenly perked up, having expected a history lesson and not such words of inspiration.

"You know your history well, for you must have been but a schoolboy when Admiral Nelson fought at Trafalgar," declared Burslem.

"How could one not know about Nelson and the Victory?" Paget asked as if assuming everyone amongst them would have intimate knowledge of the events. But he paid them no attention as he marvelled at Nelson's flagship.

The behemoth had once been a 104-gun first rate ship and the pride of the Royal Navy, but it had now been relegated to the roll of a troop ship, carrying soldiers to Portugal, and only her gun boats ever seeing action as she sailed with the convoys. Victory was in a sorry state, but to Paget she was still a great hero of the war to be revered now as the day she returned triumphant from Trafalgar, of which she was not in significantly better condition.

The port was alive with activity, making Lisbon look positively calm as ships came and went with many warships moored up and several in dry dock. It took quite some time for the Minerva to be brought up to the dock at a snail's pace, but they watched the crew work with much efficiency and skill as heaving lines were carried to the dock and tied to hawsers, the far larger and heavier ropes which were then used to haul the frigate into position. It was a tedious operation which Craven did not envy. For he was accustomed to coming and going to different locations with such ease, and it did not endear him to the sea life any. Yet as he watched the crew work, he remembered the previous days fondly as they had contested with one another in good spirits. To their amazement a crowd was gathering at the docks, and they cheered ever more loudly.

"What is that frightful noise for?" Craven asked Burslem.

"Crowds gather to celebrate their heroes."

"Do you always get such a welcome?"

"They are not here for us."

Craven looked confused, and Burslem had to go on and explain.

"Stories of your great adventures have reached those back home. It started as rumours by crews returning here. At first, I did not believe them myself, but then more reliable news began to reach Portsmouth, and it became apparent that the audacious Captain Craven was indeed real, and so were many of his exploits. You have gained some fame here, Captain. Enjoy it."

Paget could hardly believe what he was hearing, as if a dream had come true. He had always wanted to return home triumphantly to a great crowd just like Caesar had done, celebrated for his great victories. The gangplank was soon touching English soil, and Craven led the Salfords onto the dock to the roar of the crowd. Almost two hundred people had gathered so greet them, both civilians and soldiers and sailors alike. It was a magnificent display, and in the eyes of Paget it was far greater still, as if they marched to the applause of thousands as he revelled in the moment. People reached out to touch Craven and his comrades as they cheered with excitement, and children screamed at having caught a glimpse of the returning heroes.

"They love us!" Moxy cried excitedly.

Hunt revelled in it more than any of them, despite not having witnessed nor contributed to any of the actions which had brought them fame. But nobody protested as they were just swallowed up in the excitement and jubilation. It was such an extreme departure from the life they had lived in Portugal that few could find words as they walked through the crowds. Craven turned back to Captain Burslem, having left without a word, which would be a great disrespect to the ship's Captain. But he did not mind, for he now had some idea of the hardships Craven and his comrades had endured to reach this point. He waved a friendly salute as he watched Craven leave. Paget had gotten so caught up in the pageantry he had forgotten his closest friend, who he now caught a glimpse of being dangled in the air by ropes and pulleys. He turned back and pushed his way through the crowds.

"Come on, Lieutenant!" Ferreira called to him.

But he would not hear it as he went to Augustus to see he received the finest treatment. Craven had not even notice him leave as he enjoyed the impromptu parade and celebrations. He wandered on through the jubilant masses before the crowd opened up before him to a tavern. A man waited there with glass beer mugs in hand, filled to the top and waiting for him like a grail at the end of a great quest. He felt as though he were in a dream as he approached them, and yet Archie rushed ahead and grabbed the first before Craven took the other.

"Captain Craven, drinks on the house for you and all your company this day. Get your fill. For heroes will be made most welcome here!" roared the landlord.

It was yet more joy to his ears as he took his fill and took up the offer. He stepped inside, and the crowds piled in after him to hear his stories; the landlord knowing he would make far more from the people which followed him than even the thirstiest soldiers could down in one night. Craven slumped down, glad to be on solid ground and almost feeling a little sick for a moment to not be swaying in every moment. But platters of food followed the beer and soon settled his stomach, as he forgot all his woes and celebrated with a great feast fit for a king.

"Is England always so merry?" Ferreira sat down beside him.

"No, it isn't, but enjoy it whilst you can."

The tavern was bustling all day and evening as the crowd merely wanted to be in the presence of Craven and his Salfords, eagerly engaging every one of them in deep conversation. They seemingly found themselves fascinated by even the most mundane conversation and retelling of their adventures. Even Birback had a body of men enthralled in his tales as though he were a great orator. For several hours the beer and food flowed, and the conversation was deafening until finally Paget had heard enough. For him it was all so overwhelming, and he stepped outside to catch a breath of fresh air and get a little peace, to find Charlie had followed him.

"It is not the return to England you wanted?"

"It is better than I could have dreamed it, but there is a lot to be said for a few quiet moments to collect one's thoughts."

"I can leave you in peace?"

"No, I never grow tired of your company," he smiled.

They began to walk together along the waterfront, looking out across the calm port. The great tall ships loomed in the bay, lit up by a great many lanterns lurking in the shadows as menacing silhouettes out to the horizon towards France. A land Paget knew they would eventually have to travel to, which was a terrifying thought having seen how bravely French troops fought whilst abroad. He could only imagine how fearsome they might be in defence of their homeland. She wanted to embrace him, and yet could not for her identity was a very closely guarded secret which she could not risk. She knew all too well the risks of doing so and how much danger it brought to those around her.

"What is on your mind?"

"I am not even sure. I am just lost in all of this."

"How so?"

"It is not the first time I have been away from England, but I have never returned like this. Nor has it ever been so long. My family would always be awaiting me, and I feel as if I should inform them of my arrival, and yet.."

"You don't want to?"

"I am not the man who shipped out to Portugal."

"None of us are as we were," she admitted.

"But I still have duty."

"To whom?"

"To my father and to the rest of my family."

"You do not rely on them anymore. You left England as a boy, but you come back a hero."

"And yet I cannot help but feel if that were true, we would never have left."

"No one wanted to stay more than I, for I would have us seek out the French every single day I still draw breath, but Matthys is right. We cannot fight every day, and the war will not suddenly end because we are not there to fight it."

"When did you discover such wisdom," smiled Paget.

"Like I said, none of us are what we once were. I imagine if you returned to your father, he would not even recognise you."

"I am not sure that is a good thing," admitted Paget.

"Why? Have you not become what you always dreamed of being?"

"I imagined myself leading a company of one of the great

regiments of foot by now."

"That was the old you. Is that even you anymore?"

"It would please my father, but I could not achieve a quarter of what I have with a company of the finest men in the army as I have at Craven's side. The Captain is an awful officer but a great warrior, and one cannot deny his results, and yet my father would find a way."

"You stepped out of your father's shadow a long time ago, and what you have become should make any father proud, and if he cannot see that, then no matter, for you have us."

They were endearing words, but Paget could not let go of his fears of what his father might think. As he reflected on all he had seen and done, he realised just how judgemental his father would be if he learnt anything of the man he had come to follow.

* * *

There was a crash as a chair fell, and a man staggered onto a table of the tavern, spilling half of his beer in the process before getting upright as he addressed the crowd.

"To Captain of the Salford Rifles!"

He threw up his glass and spilt yet more, and yet the landlord did not protest. The man would soon have to pay to fill it back up. The roar of the excited crowds was soon followed by many more drinks downed in an instant, and he smiled at the money he was making from the rowdy gathering. It was all in a day's work for the landlord, who was accustomed to making a fortune from the crew of so many ships which moored or docked at the port. He knew a little rowdiness as worth a lot in profit, and he watched with glee as a dozen men called for fresh drinks.

Craven got his fill and enjoyed every moment of it. He ate meat off the bone and washed it down with beer which tasted the best that had ever touched his lips. He knew that was likely not true, but he was carried away and immersed in the great celebration almost as if the war were over. Though that was the last thing he wanted, for he did not want to return to a poor travelling gladiator surviving on scraps. He looked around at the great festivities all around him and took a moment to enjoy it, remembering how few days could be so good.

Despite all the loud conversation and laughter, he finally had some time where he was not being hassled by strangers to regal them of his adventures.

"I see Timmerman's influence has not reached England." Ferreira took a seat beside him.

"Clearly not, and I shouldn't imagine it would. Perhaps those at court might talk amongst themselves, but it does the country no good to hear of infighting and cowardice. The people of England must constantly be reminded what a heroic endeavour this war is."

"And let them, for it is to our advantage," smiled Ferreira.

The strangers treated him as a British officer. For amongst the hugely varied uniforms of the British Army, they had no inkling as to him wearing a Portuguese one. It did not occur to many that a man wearing a uniform and a sword on the streets of England would be anything but in the service of the English Crown.

"More beer!" Craven roared.

He had forgotten how much he had missed English ale. It

was so rarely available abroad where he had to sustain himself on Portuguese and Spanish wine, port, and madeira. It was no hardship, but it warmed his heart to sip on the bitter ales he had grown up drinking in bars across all of the British Isles.

"It was hard to drag you away from Lisbon. You were hateful at the prospect, and now look at you," declared Ferreira.

"There is still business to attend to in Lisbon, and some of it filthy business. I will not forget, but I cannot deny it is a welcome thing to step away from it. For grudges need not be settled immediately."

"You heard Major Spring. This is some time for those in Lisbon to calm themselves and forget this business with Colonel Bevan, and you must do the same."

"Must?" Craven responded angrily.

"Would you have us all go down with the Colonel? A man who is dead and done now."

Craven groaned as he knew there was some truth to it.

"Even if I could, Timmerman has stirred up many against us, and he will continue to whip them into a frenzy. If Spring thinks the angry mob in Lisbon will forget, he is gravely mistaken."

"And yet those in Spain could forget. We fought alongside our Spanish brothers only months after blockading their ports. Only a few short years after Nelson and the Victory tore through the Spanish fleet. After all that, they now fight beside you as brothers."

"You call the Spaniards your brothers?" Craven was astonished.

"Many of them are now, just as you and I. Old arguments are forgotten. Did Spain not try to invade England not so long ago?"

"Over two hundred years ago?" Craven smiled.

"My point still stands. We cannot hold onto bitter anger forever, not any of us, for it will consume us all."

"What if it is not our choice? I did not look for a fight in Lisbon, but it was Timmerman's anger which lit that fire. Even if we can forget, what if he cannot?"

"If you do not fuel a fire, it will eventually go out."

Craven smiled, as he did not believe it.

"When we return to my country, it will be to resume this war, and men will have much more to worry about than you and Colonel Bevan. This will be forgotten. It has to be."

The door to the bar was suddenly flung open, and a deeply concerned Paget filled the doorway, looking back and forth in a panic. He'd taken a blow to the eye and was cut and bruised, though nothing life threatening.

"Here we go," sighed Craven.

He soon spotted the Captain and rushed to his table.

"Sir, Sir," he gasped, having clearly run to the bar.

"What is it?" Craven groaned.

"It's Birback, Sir. He's in trouble."

"Of course, he is. He's drunk and back home."

"No, Sir, he has got himself into a lot of trouble."

"Then he can get himself back out of it. He is quite capable of handling himself. We are not at war anymore. He can handle a few ruffians."

"But, Sir…"

"But nothing! This is our first day back in England for a few years, and I will not have him ruin it."

Paget looked even more flustered than when he had burst

through the doors and looked to Ferreira for aid.

"The problems of Englishmen are not mine," he said, refusing to help.

Paget staggered back, stunned by the unwillingness to help. For now, they were away from the war it seemed as though everything was different. Charlie and Matthys approached him to help.

"You said you would return to the bar, where did you go?" Charlie demanded.

"I found Birback. He is in trouble."

Matthys looked to Craven to do something, but he would not even meet his glance.

"Where?" Matthys asked, knowing he would have to go himself.

"I can show you."

"No, let Charlie see to that cut, just tell me where he is," growled Matthys angrily.

He stormed out of the bar after getting the information he needed. Nobody followed him, either not noticing him leave or not caring to get involved. They all knew Birback had a tendency to get himself into trouble, and he usually deserved it, and yet he always managed to find his way out the other side in defiance of the odds. But Matthys would not leave one of their own to face danger alone. He jogged along the route Paget had told him, and soon enough he could hear a great ruckus. He turned a bend into a small square to find a great brawl underway. Around twenty men were brawling in an out-of-control exchange with Birback at the centre. Most seemed to be focusing their attention on the burly and angry drunken Scotsman, but he swung in heavy blows, knocking two to the ground as Matthys watched on.

"Birback!" Matthys shouted in his Sergeant's voice, expecting to call him to attention, and yet knowing there was no chance of it.

But then he noticed one of the men had a large knife in hand and another beat down against Birback with a heavy cudgel, first knocking his arm down and then smashing him in the head. Matthys approached as the knifeman closed with Birback. The Sergeant grabbed at his sword hand and locked it with his left, dealing a heavy punch into the man's temple. It caused him to stagger away and release the weapon, which Matthys caught before launching it into a building frame well above any of their reach. Birback's attackers backed away a little as Matthys took up position beside him, preparing for war. He hated that it had come to this, but he would not see Birback murdered in the street.

"This is over. Leave us!" Birback ordered.

"Not until he pays what he owes!" roared someone in the mob.

Five men lay unconscious or unable to get to their feet where Birback had smashed them with his fists, and yet there were still eight more ready to do battle. Birback smiled as if enjoying every minute whilst blood trickled down from his open head wound.

"Come on!"

"No, stop!" Matthys cried out, but it was too late.

The mob rushed towards them, and Matthys had no choice but to defend himself. He started swinging his fists to try and even up the odds before they were overwhelmed. Blow after blow was delivered, and he felt one body blow crack one of his ribs. He winced in pain but fought it off as he kept swinging, but the sound of the watchmen's rattles echoed out with a loud clattering sound to alert more of their kind to the trouble.

Matthys watched in horror as six men in thick long coats and wielding lanterns and staffs stormed onto the scene. They began to beat on all those who were engaged in the melee without mercy or care for who was to blame or who was attacking who. They suppressed the fighting men as cavalry scattered wavering infantry on the battlefield. Several of those attacking Birback and Matthys fled, but the others continued their battle, and even took the fight to the watchmen with no respect for their authority.

Birback had not shown any care for their arrival, perhaps assuming they were on his side, considering he and Matthys still wore their soldier's coats, but they beat down against all involved in the fray without care. One struck Matthys on the knee, and he dropped down before another stick beat down on his head and he collapsed.

"Wait!" Matthys held up his hands, not wanting to fight against the watchmen who patrolled the streets and maintained order. But they were used to dealing with rowdy drunks, mischievous sailors, and troublemaking soldiers, and they showed no restraint at all. A watchman's staff crashed down onto Matthys' head, and he dropped unconscious to the ground.

CHAPTER 10

Craven awoke feeling dry and weak and with a throbbing headache, and yet he could not help but smile as he thought back to the night of festivities. The fresh and energised feelings whilst aboard the Minerva had already been long forgotten. He had been encouraged to descend into a drunken stupor and had wholeheartedly embraced it, having been offered free quarters above the tavern, the owner knowing that having the Captain under his roof would continue to bring in a stream of curious customers. He staggered downstairs and was offered more food and some wine, this time without even having asked for it. He took it gladly, for it felt good to be waited upon and treated like royalty.

"Why, oh, why did we not come back to England sooner?" he smiled as Ferreira asked for some food and grumbled about being asked to pay for it.

"You almost had to be dragged aboard a ship to leave my

country," he groaned as he sat down.

"I don't remember it being such a hospitable place," he smiled as he took his fill.

"Fame can go a long way, but don't get used to it, for it doesn't last," muttered Ferreira.

"How would you know?"

Ferreira grimaced at his tone, but he knew he had a point. He never got such treatment back home. His return to Lisbon had been an uneventful affair, and it was his home city.

"This is not even your home city, is it?"

"Oh, no."

"And where is that?"

"I don't even know anymore," admitted Craven. He had been on the road for so long, he wasn't even sure what to call home anymore.

"You grew up near Hawkshaw, so you have a home?"

"My father's home, not mine," snarled Craven.

Ferreira dared not delve any deeper because it was clearly a sore subject. His food soon arrived on a plate half the size of Craven's. He looked disgruntled and soon finished up before heading for the door.

"I am going for a walk. I did not come all the way to England to waste my days in the tavern."

"Really? It's the best we have to offer," smiled Craven.

Ferreira wasn't even sure if he was joking. He seemed to be slipping back into some old behaviours with the comfort of England, far from the dangers of Napoleon's armies, and the orders of Wellington who had kept him on a precise course since their first encounter.

"Are you really going to sit here in this dark dungeon

whilst the sun shines?"

"I've spent the last two years on the road throughout Portugal and Spain. I just got the opportunity to put my feet up and enjoy free food and beer, why would I go anywhere?"

"Perhaps there is more to life than wine and food?"

Craven gave an exhausted sigh.

"I've spent my whole life seeing new places, up and down the whole country. There is not a corner I have not seen, and I have spent the last two years doing much the same in Portugal and Spain. If I'm not being paid to move, then I'm not moving."

"Suit yourself, but we have time on our hands far away from war, and I intend to make some use of it." He gathered up his hat and sword and walked out. Gamboa stopped a moment as if to ask permission.

"What are you waiting for? Go on!" Craven yelled at him.

The Lieutenant followed on after Ferreira. The two Portuguese officers set out to see England for themselves, a country they had heard so much about. None more so than from Paget who would spend endless hours regaling anyone who would listen of his home country's beauty. Craven went on eating and drinking and answered the questions of all who came looking to meet him. He was basking in the moment, drawing more attention than he ever had as a professional gladiator.

It was the middle of the afternoon when Paget finally staggered into the room and sat down beside him. His head was bandaged from the knock he had taken the night before, and he still looked dazed. He reached for the bandage and seemed surprised to discover it there as if he had little memory of the night before.

"Looks like you had a good night," Craven smiled at him.

"I…I am not sure, Sir."

Charlie joined them as she passed some water to the Lieutenant.

"You came to find the Colonel because Birback had gotten himself in trouble, remember?"

Paget could not, but as he sipped on the water, some memories began to come back to him.

"Yes, Birback fell in with some awful men. They accused him of stealing from them, and he of them cheating him in a game or something."

"That sounds about right. Though our Birback was not likely the innocent party," replied Craven.

"I tried to help but I was thrown aside and struck my head on something," pondered Paget.

"You should have left him to it."

"I came looking for your help, Sir, and you refused. And Captain Ferreira, too."

"Birback is a damned fool. He got himself into trouble like he always does, but we are home now, and he is not my problem," groaned Craven.

"But he is one of us," pleaded Paget.

Yet Craven was not interested and did not want to hear it.

"Sergeant Matthys, yes, Matthys the kind soul, he went to help Birback. I tried to go after him, but my legs were week, and I was in no condition for it."

Craven went on drinking without a care.

"Did they come back?"

Craven shrugged.

"I have no idea where they made lodgings."

"Sergeant Matthys would have returned here before the

night was through. He would not leave without a word," insisted Paget.

Craven shrugged once more, but Paget shot up, and he threw his chair back, causing it to crash down on the floor.

"You should rest easy," insisted Charlie.

"Not until I know the whereabouts and condition of Sergeant Matthys and Birback."

He turned and left as Charlie looked to Craven for support.

"What? He can do as he pleases."

Charlie huffed angrily before rushing on after him, not wanting to leave him to wander the streets alone with a head injury.

"Can't sit down for five minutes, can they?" Hunt asked as he and Craven had a good laugh about it.

Charlie stormed on after Paget who had made some significant distance considering his injury and dazed state.

"Where are you going?"

"To look for them."

"But where?"

"The last place I saw Birback. That is where we must start."

They rushed on as he tried to retrack his steps, having to go back on himself several times. He finally stepped into a square where several men were busy repairing market stall tables and chairs which had recently been damaged.

"This is the place," he insisted.

"Are you sure?" Charlie could see no sign of either of the men.

"I am sure, this is where the fight took place."

"You're right about that," groaned one of the men working on repairs.

"Go on," pressed Paget.

"There was quite a fight here last night. I heard a great big giant of a man got into it after a game of cards. The giant certainly tore up the place and gave those local boys some trouble."

"And where are they now? Tell me!"

"The night watchmen dealt with them. I should imagine they are locked up in a gaol."

"And where would that be?"

The man shrugged, but a sailor walking past piped up.

"If your man was in uniform, he was probably taken to Broke's Gaolhouse."

"Why there?"

"A man trained in arms and encouraged to use them can be quite the handful, Sir," replied the sailor to the laughter of his comrades.

"It is a rough place, then?" Charlie asked.

"The worst," added the sailor.

"Where can I find this gaolhouse?" Paget asked.

* * *

The sun had gone down and Craven had been drinking throughout the day, but he kept on going. He and Hunt roared with laughter as they kept on drinking and playing cards with some common sailors, tossing coins about as if they were nothing. Craven had returned with a respectable purse of money and had no expenses of his own. Unlike anyone who was locked up in a gaolhouse, who was expected to pay an entrance fee and daily costs for their upkeep, condemning some who could not pay for release to be incarcerated for the rest of their days. Craven did not yet know of any incarnation of his comrades, but he was about to find out. Paget and Charlie stepped into the bar, eagerly searching for him in a replay of the night before, and this time Craven looked even more exhausted by the prospect of Paget hounding him.

"What is it this time?"

"Birback, Sir, he is locked in a gaolhouse."

"Of course, he is," sighed Craven.

"But not just him, Sir, Sergeant Matthys also."

"Matthys?" Craven looked to Hunt who burst out into laughter, as he imagined the embarrassment the pious Sergeant would be feeling. Craven quickly went back to his game, tossing a few more coins into the middle of the table.

"What will you do, Sir?"

"Do?"

"You have to help them, Sir."

"Why? Why do I have to help them? This is not a war. They are not captured by the enemy. They are sobering up in the gaolhouse because they went looking for trouble and they found it," snarled Craven.

"Sir? Birback perhaps, but Matthys? He only went to help because I asked it of him. And that was because you would not help, nor Captain Ferreira."

Craven looked increasingly frustrated, wanting to get on with enjoying himself.

"Must Captain Craven be responsible for everyone all the

time?" Hunt asked.

"Yes, for that is his duty."

"If that were true, would those under his command also not have a responsibility to keep their behaviour in check?"

Paget stuttered as he tried to respond.

"An officer's job is to protect his men from the enemy and maintain discipline. Perhaps a few days in the gaolhouse will be a lesson to them both," added Hunt.

Paget looked furious, but Craven was indifferent. He was having far too much fun and didn't want to stop.

"Sir? Will you abandon our men now when they need you?"

"I have not abandoned anyone, Mr Paget. In fact, they have abandoned me. For they have gotten themselves into this trouble and robbed me of two soldiers. Perhaps Captain Hunt is right. Maybe they will learn a lesson here."

Paget tried to go forward and speak again, but Charlie held his arm back and shook her head, pleading with him to stop. She pulled him to one side where they could talk quietly.

"Why do you stop me now? Why not press further?"

"Because it will get you nowhere. Craven is nothing if not stubborn. Keep pressing him, and you will anger him and bring down a torrent upon your head."

"But he must help Matthys and Birback."

"He should, but nothing and nobody will force his hand."

But Paget pulled away from her, not heeding her warning. He appealed to Craven once more, who sighed in anger before he could even get a word out, and yet still he pressed forward in the only way he knew how.

"Sir, our comrades who have saved both of our lives more

than once are rotting in a cell, will you not lift a finger to help them?"

"Why? Why me? Why can you not do it. Why do you not take some of your father's precious money and buy their freedom?" Craven snapped as if angry and jealous of what Paget had been born into. It was a side of Craven he had not seen before.

"Tell me, Lieutenant? Why can you not do this? Why bother me with this?"

"Because, Sir, the gaoler knows who commands them, and he will only deal with the great Captain Craven," seethed Paget.

"Will he?" Craven laughed, "Well, Captain Hunt, what would you say we should do?"

"I'd let them rot, at least for a while."

"Let them rot," repeated Craven.

Paget's whole body dropped a few inches. He felt embarrassed and ashamed as he staggered away, as if having been beaten down by many blows, his body and heart severely mauled. Charlie felt awful for him, and yet knew she was powerless to change Craven's mind. She had tried too many times in the past to know when it was best to give up the fight. She went to the bar and put money down, asking for a bottle of whiskey and a pair of glasses. She returned to Paget and sat down opposite him. She poured out two large measures and slid one across to him.

"Here, drink," she insisted.

"Why?"

"Because this day isn't going to get any better, but I can make it go faster."

"How will that help Birback and Sergeant Matthys?"

"It won't, but it will help you. Tomorrow you can look at this fresh, but tonight the battle is over."

He begrudgingly accepted. He'd never been much of a drinker, but he was glad to feel the first whiskey calm his nerves a little and relax his body. He looked over to see Craven and Hunt having a whale of a time as they drank and gambled the night away, partying as if they had no cares in the world. Charlie put a hand over his, drawing his eyes away from Craven's table as she tried to find some words to console him.

"You did what you could. You gave it everything. Sometimes that isn't enough, no matter who you are and no matter how much effort you give. Today's battle is over, but we live to fight another day."

The sentiment was appreciated. He had felt the same many times before, glad to have his own life and knowing he could try again and do better in the future. The whiskey flowed quickly, and his worries soon faded to a fraction of what they were. Although, when he got up to go to his bed for the night, he could see and hear Craven and Hunt partying more brashly and loudly than ever. But Charlie soon gave him a prod, encouraging him on towards his bed. He lay down but he could hear the roar of Craven's laughter even through the floorboards, but Charlie had been right. The night had gone quicker, and he was now so tired he could not keep his eyes open and angrily stew over the situation any longer.

He woke up feeling surprisingly fresh, and with some surprise by all of the noise and bustle out on the street for a moment he had forgotten where he was. He got up and went to the window to look out across the port. All the recent events were coming flooding back to him, including the frustrating night before. He put on his jacket but only half buttoned it up, not finding the motivation to maintain his usual standards as he went down to the bar to find some breakfast. He noticed Ferreira and Gamboa digging into a meal of their own, but he chose to sit far from them, having found no more support from Ferreira than from Craven when he needed it on the night of Birback's battle.

But as Ferreira heard the young Lieutenant's voice ring out, he spotted him and moved over with his plate in hand to join him.

"You look a little worse for wear," he smiled.

"Not half as bad as those in gaol," retorted Paget.

"Gaol? Who?"

It dawned on Paget that neither of the Portuguese officers knew of the developments he had discovered. Before Paget could reply, the rowdy Craven and Hunt staggered down the stairs to find some food. Paget held his tongue as they passed the table, and that made Ferreira even more curious to know more.

"Well? Speak up," he insisted.

But Paget still looked weary as he looked over towards Craven as if not wanting to betray him. Yet the Captain showed no interest at all as he chatted and laughed with Hunt as they relived the previous evenings shenanigans.

"Sir, Birback and Sergeant Matthys are being held in a gaol following a fight over some gambling dispute."

"Since when?"

"From the first night we arrived here in Portsmouth."

"Why hasn't someone secured their release?" Ferreira demanded angrily.

"Their gaoler will not release them to anyone but Captain Craven."

"And you have told Craven about this?"

"I have."

"And?" Ferreira became more interested as to his response.

"The Captain would do nothing. He said to let them rot. He would have them taught a lesson."

"He what?" Ferreira looked over to the Captain with disgust, and Gamboa also looked on in disbelief.

"Why is this the first I am hearing of it?"

"I came to you, Sir, when Birback was in trouble, but you did not want to know. You told me the problems of Englishmen were not yours. I did not have the heart to remind you that Birback is a Scot."

Ferreira looked frustrated that he had been away and missed so much, as well as for having shown so little care himself. He had never thought the situation would devolve so badly.

"What will you do, Sir?" Paget was clearly greatly concerned about the matter.

Ferreira cast his chair back and stormed over to Craven's table.

"Good morning, Captain, did you enjoy the sights of Portsmouth?" Craven asked him.

"Why will you not lift a finger when two of your own are in gaol?"

Craven was taken aback by Ferreira's aggressive tone and so glared at him in disbelief.

"Two of your men are behind bars, including one who has

been there for you in your worst days, and yet you will not lift a finger to help him?"

Craven still said nothing, and Ferreira was almost panting with rage.

"I demand that you go and see to the release of these two men!"

His voice carried across the whole bar. All were silenced and watched intently as the situation unfolded.

"You demand?"

"You will go and secure their release, or you will answer to me," snarled Ferreira.

"I answer to nobody but Wellington!" Craven responded arrogantly.

"Then I will see you outside, and we will settle this. For I demand satisfaction."

Ferreira rushed to the door and drew out his sword.

"Calm down, you stupid fool," Craven shouted after him without even getting up off his chair.

"I will not. For it is you who is acting the fool and forgetting your responsibility. Get out here, now!"

Ferreira burst through the doors and out into the daylight. The bar was still silent as all stared at Craven. He looked to Archie who would not get involved. Craven knew he could not do nothing, and so he rose up and walked out to join Ferreira. The bar emptied to follow him. They gathered outside, but Craven would not draw his sword as the audience formed around them like an arena.

"What is this? What has gotten into you?"

Ferreira was seething and shaking with rage in a way none of them had seen him since his feud with Braganza. Paget watched on in horror, praying nothing would come of it, and yet also desperately wanting an outcome to the sad affair of Matthys and Birback.

"Above all else we have a duty and a responsibility to one another. It is the reason we have survived this long. It is the reason we have achieved great things, and it is the reason we can keep on moving forward. I never thought I would see the day that James Craven would not fight for his friends!"

"Would you tell me how to command the Salfords? Do you think you know better?"

"I know men follow you because they know you will have their backs, and if that has changed, then you are no better than the worst bastards who bought their commission to prance about and play at being a soldier."

"And you would fight me for it? Knowing you cannot win?"

"I don't want to fight you, Craven, but if it is the fire lit under your arse to do the right thing, then I will do it. First blood of the torso, and if I win, you go and set our men free!"

"And if I win? And I will," growled Craven.

"Then I will hold my tongue, but you will still be a fool."

Craven was angered enough to finally draw his sword as the two peeled away their jackets. Ferreira passed his to Paget, who was more accustomed to taking Craven's before such a contest, and he could not help but notice the oddity in the reversal.

"Don't kill him," whispered Paget.

Ferreira smirked, for he knew he was not nearly as skilled and would be fighting against heavy odds, despite all he had learned.

Nobody tried to intervene with the fight, and many passers-by even came to join the crowd, eager for some action before their eyes. Craven looked weary and hungover and yet ever dangerous, whilst Ferreira was fresh and invigorated by his cause. It was the last thing he imagined himself doing in England, but he could not let Paget down, not now. The two Captains came to their guards, knowing they risked death as they clashed with the weapons that they used in war, the swords which had been the end of many a Frenchman.

Ferreira started the engagement with several short and snappy thrusts delivered as feints. Craven looked slow compared to his normal self but still very capable. He moved to defend each one without creating any large openings to strike. Ferreira quickly followed with cuts, drawing Craven's guard out further. As Craven returned a thrust which would have pierced his breast, the Portuguese Captain dropped very low beneath the blade. Yet he did not land a thrust to the torso as he knew he could have, for it could have been fatal. Instead, he cut across the top of Craven's thigh, opening his breeches and a long but shallow cut.

Craven shrugged off the blow as if it were nothing, not willing to accept or admit that Ferreira had gone easy on him for the love they shared. But Craven was in a frenzy now as he went forward to prove himself. He struck wildly and yet with power. Ferreira was forced to retreat until finally he missed a parry and was cut on the forearm. Craven smiled at his small victory before they reset to their guard positions. Craven began to launch far more precise feints now. He grew in strength and speed with every blow, the adrenaline pumping about his body countering his hangover and lethargic state. He was returning to the Craven they all knew, at least as a fighter if not a man. Ferreira began to struggle and was cut again across the upper arm before the two locked up close in a standing grapple.

"No! Stop this!"

Paget rushed in and tried to force the two of them apart as he could not take it any longer. He struggled with the size and weight of the two men who seemed to only care for their bloodlust. Finally, he shoved them apart, but Craven dealt a lashing cut as Ferreira spun away and instead caught Paget on the side of the head, opening up a long cut. The Lieutenant was frozen by the blow as the two fighters stopped and looked in horror.

"Paget?" Craven shouted, having broken out of his fury, genuinely concerned.

The young man fell to the floor as Craven threw away his sword and rushed to catch him before his head struck the hard ground. He was bleeding profusely from the head wound. Craven looked up in despair at Ferreira, as if a switch had been flicked and he had become the man they all knew and loved.

"Help me," he pleaded with Ferreira, who also let go of his sword and rushed to Paget's side. They lifted him up and carried him to the bar. They laid the Lieutenant down on a chair as Ferreira placed a cloth against his head, and Craven knelt down before him.

"You are going to be okay, you will make it," insisted Craven.

Paget looked weak but as determined as ever.

"Promise me you will see to their release?" he demanded.

Craven looked to Ferreira, both terrified they might have caused the young officer's demise.

"You have my word," replied Craven soberly.

CHAPTER 11

Craven looked every bit the outcast as he sat alone watching a Royal Navy Surgeon see to Paget's wounds in the very same bar where he had first come to ask for help. In hindsight, he could see now that it could all have been avoided, and Charlie glared at him with furious anger. None of them talked to him except Hunt and Hawkshaw, and that made him feel even more isolated, as the British officer class watched from afar with an air of both authority and arrogance, which established a 'them and us' class which he had never wanted.

"All is well in the end, ey?" Hunt asked as if brushing it all off.

"All is not well," muttered Craven.

"But it will be in time, this can be undone," insisted Hawkshaw who was rather more sympathetic to his plight.

Craven looked deeply saddened to see Paget in such a state, having received two head wounds in as many days, and one of them by his hand. It made him feel a little sick, and then the continuous drinking since they had arrived did not help. Hunt offered him a bottle of wine, but he turned it away and shot to his feet. He went towards Paget to talk with him man to man. He stopped two yards short and tried to find his words.

"That will be quite the scar," he finally blurted out.

Paget's wound extended from within his hair line and several inched down his face over his cheek bone just in front of his right eye.

"It will look most dashing, though I must admit I wish I had a better story to tell of how I earned it."

"You don't need it, for you have plenty of great stories of better days," replied Craven solemnly before both of them fell silent, and Craven tried to find his words.

He looked to Charlie, seeing her furious eyes demanded a lot. She looked as though she was ready to come for his blood if he did not speak in a way which met with her approval, and more importantly, with Paget's. He looked back to the Lieutenant as his wound was finally sewn up and the Surgeon finished his work.

"How can I make this right?" Craven asked in a genuine and apologetic tone.

Ferreira was a few yards away and turned in amazement to hear the conversation going on. All were silent as they waited to hear Paget's demands, knowing he held all the cards and could demand almost anything from Craven.

"I only want what I have always wanted, to know the soldiers either side of me have my back and would not hesitate to fight for me, just as I will fight for them. You talk of a brotherhood between us, but will you fight for your brothers or are they just words?"

Craven was now humbled even more. He felt foolish, but he knew what he must do.

"Let's go and get our brothers," he declared.

A cheer rang out as many about them sprang to their feet. Paget got up and closed the distance with Craven so he could talk more privately.

"Don't forget who your brothers are, Sir. For you ask everything of them, and they should rightfully expect just as much in return."

* * *

Matthys was seething. He had been sitting on the opposite side of the same small cell as Birback since their incarceration, but he had said nothing. He was angry, and yet he tried desperately to hold his tongue and not lash out like so many others would. He was a considerate and caring man, but even he could take so much. The men they had battled with sat along the walls between them. It was a filthy cell with little space to move about. Both of them looked worse for wear, with dried blood on their faces and uniform and various bruises. Matthys felt as though he had been through Talavera once again, worse even. Finally, he could hold his tongue no further.

"Why, oh, why can you not stay out of trouble?" he asked as he was starting to shake with anger.

"That's my business. You didn't have to get involved," replied Birback unapologetically.

"Yes, I did, because we are in this together. When are you

going to get that through your thick skull?"

It was the angriest he had ever seen Matthys, and yet he didn't understand why he was so furious.

"We are not in battle here. We are not even in Portugal or Spain, so what is it to you?" he replied in his defence.

"Until one of us takes the uniform off, it is everything. We have each other's back, no matter what."

"Why?"

Matthys got to his feet and slammed the wall of their cell. It was an old stone construction and part of an abandoned coach house, hundreds of years old. The roof was collapsing and much of the plaster rendering missing. Damp seeped in from every angle. There was one small window with thick iron bars and a heavy wooden door which was sealed shut.

"Can you never think of anyone but yourself?" Matthys spun around and pointed an accusatory finger at his reckless comrade in arms.

"Why would I?" he replied, without even having to think about it.

Matthys shook his head in frustration because he had seen Birback do the right and honourable thing. He knew there was some good in him, and yet far away from the war he had reverted to the base ruffian he always had been. It brought back painful memories of similar encounters years ago, long before they had set out for Portugal whilst they travelled the lands, fighting and competing in anything they could find. Matthys knew he had always been a rogue, but he seemed to have gotten worse ever since the war in Portugal and Spain, as if it had seemingly given him an unconditional licence to be a barbarian.

"Why can you just not enjoy yourself? We are back in

England, and we come back as heroes with money in our pockets."

"Yes? And how much of that do you have left? How much did you lose to this scum?" Matthys gestured towards the men they shared a cell with who until now had remained peaceful since they were put behind bars.

"Who are you calling scum?" demanded one as he shot to his feet.

"Do you think you are more? What have you ever done besides thieve and leech from this fine country?" replied Matthys angrily as he found an outlet for his anger which he struggled to continue to pile upon his brother but would gladly take it out on someone far worse. He didn't feel good about it, nor very Christian, and yet he needed it. He had festered in his fury for days and needed to let it out. Birback watched with glee as the angry ruffian squared off against the Sergeant who was a calm and considerate man, and yet a most capable fighter when he needed to be.

"You think you are a hero because you put on that uniform and took the King's shilling?" asked the ruffian.

"I suppose you are a hero for robbing men at night? Too scared to march with the army and fight a real fight. You are nothing but a coward with a bad attitude."

Birback grinned and watched with glee as the first punch was thrown towards Matthys, but the Sergeant caught it in his palm, striking back with a thunderous hook which floored his man. The rest of his friends leapt up to join in the fight, but Birback grabbed one and slammed him back against the wall before he could reach Matthys. Punches were thrown in every direction, but the door to the cell soon swung open. Two prison guards rushed in with batons to subdue them, not for any care for their prisoners, but for a desire to keep on profiting from them. The two guards began lashing their sticks at the nearest targets,

"Halt!" a booming voice roared.

Everyone froze at the sound of the commanding call which had not come from any gaoler. They all looked to the open door, as if expecting some kind of monster to step through it, and yet it was Craven with the gaol warden by his side looking a little sheepish. Craven strode in like he owned the place, not even bothering to take a weapon in hand, despite having sword, dirk, and pistol all on his belt.

"These soldiers are my own, and you will not lay another hand on them!"

The one who had started a feud with Matthys, and was clearly the ringleader, spat on the floor before him. Craven cracked a lightning-fast back fist into his face, breaking his nose as he fell back against the wall, blood streaming down his face.

"You bastard!"

The man bounced back from the wall and went forward at Craven, but the Captain quickly drew his dirk. He placed the edge against the bloody man's throat, causing him to stop instantly and recoil slightly. Craven followed him back to the wall and pinned him there with one hand whilst pressing the dagger harder into his neck. It was enough to open a tiny cut and make the man wince, but above all realise how close he was to losing his life. The prison guards laughed at the man's plight in their own sadistic way, which made Matthys feel sick and wished he had played no part in it.

"You don't lay a finger on one of my men again, or any

soldier, and if I hear that you have, I will end you. This is my word and promise as Captain James Craven of the Salford Rifles."

The name struck fear into the ruffian who stopped resisting.

"We are leaving," insisted Craven as he let the man go.

"You are free to leave," declared the gaol warden in a surprisingly civil tone after having taken from Matthys and Birback everything they had in payment for their upkeep.

Craven led them out, but as Birback left, he jabbed a quick and hard punch into the bloody man's nose, smiling at his pain in revenge for the attack two nights past. They were led out to a table full of their possessions, including the coin purse Matthys had been carrying. He was surprised to see it was full and looked to the warden who would not make eye contact with him. They gathered up their things, and despite their bedraggled state, they instantly felt more themselves as they took their personal possessions back. Craven handed them each their sword belts. Matthys looked deeply appreciative before they walked out into the freedom of the open air and took a breath of the fresh air.

"What took you so long?" Birback demanded.

"A few complications," declared Craven.

Matthys could see from the faces of those around them and Paget's wounds that there was a lot to the story, and yet he was just relieved to be free and to see them all working together.

"What now?"

"I suggest you find a bath," smiled Craven.

"And then?"

"What would you have us do?" Craven asked, knowing he needed the advice of his friend, the stalwart Sergeant who had gotten them all through the toughest of times.

"We need rest, and we need to recruit, and we cannot do that here. This port is a pit of despair and depravity, and the only good men will surely be scooped up by the Navy."

"So, what then?"

"Go North, towards familiar ground."

"This is England. It's all familiar."

"To Manchester, to where all this began," added Matthys, thinking of the militia rifle regiment which had brought them all into the service and where they had drawn the name they now carried with pride.

"The Manchester and Salfords are long gone."

"But they live on with us. Let us go home and remind all of such days," he said with hope.

Craven looked around to the others. Few were familiar with their days in the Independent Rifle militia as so many who now marched with them had been recruited abroad. It was a part of Craven's past which was rarely talked about, and yet Paget excitedly stepped forward.

"Yes, Sir, let's go to Manchester."

"You would not have us go to London?"

"I have seen quite enough of London, Sir. I have seen the finest dressed militia and yeomanry who play soldier but will never see a real battle in their lifetimes. I used to think they were the most wonderful soldiers, but now I know they are not soldiers at all. Let us go North and see where Captain Craven and the Salfords were forged."

Paget smiled and breathed a sigh of relief to see them all back together, and they were soon making their preparations to set out the next morning.

"Where are you going?" Charlie asked as she saw Paget wandering off alone.

"I will not travel through England in such a dreadful state," he declared without any more explanation.

She rushed on beside him, eager to ensure he did not go anywhere without protection. Paget led them to a military outfitter near the busiest part of the port. It was a lavish establishment, which clearly catered to the wealthy naval officers who frequently travelled through, as well as the army officers who also had to use such ports whenever leaving or returning from service abroad. Garish displays in the windows displayed beautiful swords the likes of which Charlie couldn't ever imagine taking to war. Some were even so elaborate they could no longer function as a weapon. For the grips would be uncomfortable if not dangerous to use, and the hilt fittings and scabbards were so heavy one would walk lopsided when wearing them. She stopped to marvel at them, amazed by their beauty but struggling to understand their purpose.

"Marvellous, aren't they?"

"Sort of, but how are you supposed to use them?"

"You are not."

"A sword that is not for use?"

"Yes, they are presentation swords. Given as prizes and as gifts."

"To do what with?" she asked in astonishment.

"As keepsakes, to put on display, to be given a sword is a great honour."

"If someone was to send me the gift of a sword I could not use, I would wonder at their sanity."

Paget laughed.

"Come on," he declared as he led her inside. The staff looked at the bedraggled young man as if a gift from the gods, as he was in need of many new uniform items. Yet they could tell his old, ragged attire would have cost a significant amount, though the shop workers looked down upon Charlie with contempt. A common soldier had no purpose in such an establishment, and yet they dared not say anything in the company of Paget, assuming she must have come as a mule to carry his new purchases. So, they put up with her presence for the sake of financial gain.

"What can I do for you, young Sir?" asked the shopkeeper.

"I march North on the recruiting trail, and I would look my best."

"North, Sir? Then you must be back from service abroad," said the owner politely, buttering up his customer to make him feel most at home and in the best of spirits to open his purse and spend freely.

"That's right."

"You look at though you have seen quite the battle."

Paget laughed.

"Oh, this? This did not come from battle, for this is nothing but the mundane of day-to-day service," he declared.

The shopkeeper didn't seem at all surprised to see such a young officer speak with seemingly so much experience of war. He met them every day as they came and went through Portsmouth. He helped Paget out of his old clothes, which were not really old at all, but had suffered through the frays and the fire. Paget was soon measured up and received almost everything anew, which astonished Charlie, who wore patched and faded clothing which she had grown quite attached to.

He was soon as good as new and handed over a pile of coins which made Charlie balk, for it was as much money as she had made all year. At least as much as the army had paid her, for she had taken much more from the enemy. The shopkeeper was ringing his hands with delight at the easy sales he had made, but Charlie could see the effect on Paget was worth every penny. Not because of how he looked, which was indeed very sharp, but for how it made him feel. In fact, Charlie preferred him looking as worn from campaign and battle as the rest of them, but every time he stepped into a new uniform, he seemed to stand taller and prouder like a man reborn. He stepped out into the street looking like he was ready for parade before the King.

They retired to the bar that evening, the same bar Craven had spent all his hours in, but the drinking was more restrained this time, and the Salfords were gathered together as friends once more. Matthys sat at the same table, and even if they did not speak, it was a step in the right direction.

"This Manchester, what is it like?" Ferreira asked.

"An industrial powerhouse, the industrial heart of England," replied Matthys.

"Factories and mills and filth, why would we go there?"

"Because it is a city of hope," replied Craven.

They were all surprised to hear it.

"Men and women flock to a place that grows and flourishes like that as they look to better their lives. A bustling city with much to offer."

"And you think we may recruit well there, Sir?" Paget asked.

"Undoubtedly, for a soldier's life is half the work they are used to!" Craven's answer drew plenty of laughter.

Those who had witnessed the factory life knew it to be true. It was backbreaking labour, often from dawn until dusk and frequently no safer than going off to war. Paget had no concept of such a hard existence, but if it was once home to their namesake regiment, he was eager to see the place where it all began.

"To the Salford Rifles!" Craven lifted his glass to a roar of support from all.

The morning came quickly, and they were all fresh and eager to move on and away from the chaos of Portsmouth. Even Craven who had lived rent and board for free had grown tired of it, though he would miss the endless free drinks more than anything. They set out on horseback, and it felt like they went on for another adventure, and yet this time it was not toward the enemy and great danger.

It was a beautiful English summer's day, warm but not intoxicating nor with any significant humidity. Ferreira couldn't help but look impressed as they rode North through Winchester and on toward Oxford and great green fields and forests as far as the eye could see. It was a lush and rich countryside, which Gamboa could only have dreamed of before seeing it with his own eyes.

"Is this what you came for?" Ferreira asked him.

"It was certainly worth it if nothing else. I never thought I would leave our country. I imagined I would be born, live, and die there just as my father and his father before him. But this, what a beautiful country."

Paget was amused as the Portuguese officer spoke of his homeland just as he did theirs, marvelling at the beauty of foreign lands as if they were painted by the most skilled and imaginative artists in the world. Farmers laboured across the lands as they rode on through, but they looked far better dressed and wealthier than the shoeless and ragged peasants who so often worked the Portuguese fields.

"This is a most rich country."

"Rich far beyond our land, and yet most of the people still live an abhorrent life," replied Ferreira.

"I don't know, it does not look a bad one to my eyes," replied Gamboa.

"Wait until you see what the cities have become, for they are like nothing you can imagine!" Craven asked.

"They are not beautiful?"

Craven laughed as he remembered the stink of Lisbon with fond memories, for it was far more inviting than the intoxicating fumes of an industrial powerhouse full of mills and factories.

"Manchester is a shithole, but a good shithole," replied Birback.

The group roared with laughter, and Matthys looked about in amazement to see they were all in good spirits. It was all he could have asked for, though he wished it could have come sooner. For they could have ridden North and avoided all the chaos Portsmouth had caused them, or perhaps they had brought upon themselves. They rode on through the day before Craven led them off the road to a quiet spot beside some trees to settle in for the night. It was a surprise to them all, as every road was littered with inns and taverns to provide comforts to those on the road.

"We sleep under the stars, Sir?" Paget asked in surprise.

"It was good enough for us in Spain, and it will be good

enough for us here in England."

Ferreira grumbled, as he didn't see any reason to slum it now they were in a safe country and with money in their pockets, but Matthys soon came to his side to discourage him from protesting.

"We need this, Captain, away from the chaos. From the drunken card games and petty squabbles. A return to a simpler time."

"A bed is a pretty simple request," he groaned.

But he smiled as he patted Matthys on the back, appreciating the sentiment as the Sergeant worked to keep the unit together as it fractured at the seams. It was a good day, and they could all feel it as they settled in for the night with not a single protest about their rough sleeping conditions. They were merely glad to be moving forward and not be at each other's throats.

CHAPTER 12

The drum beat and the Sergeant's voice roared as he marched his recruiting party through a small village, drawing excited children and young men to the fanfare. The Sergeant had a perpetual smile on his face, as though he had the best job in the world and promised army life would be everything every enthusiastic young man would imagine it would be. It was not long before he had recruits signing on for the 23rd Foot, the Welch Fusiliers. They were a long way from their barracks, and yet that is how recruitment worked now. No longer did regiments recruit only in their home counties, but wherever they were stationed, and wherever their recruiting parties marched, which was far and wide across the lands.

It was a marvellous and fascinating sight for the Portuguese officers to behold, for they had never seen anything like it. The militias required compulsory service in their country, and the army was seen as a necessity by many to either earn a respectable wage or in defence of their country against Napoleon; a threat which had loomed over them long before he ever marched his armies into their country. Matthys watched the recruiting Sergeant with both amazement and disgust, for he was both very good at his job but also incredibly devious, doing whatever he must do to get recruits no matter what lies he had to tell.

"All of that really works. Men believe it?" Gamboa asked.

"Of course, they do, because they want to. The same way any man wants to believe the most wonderous story you tell them," Matthys replied.

He even felt a little envious as he could see fit and enthusiastic young men who could be of great use to the Salfords, but they were signing up with ease to the recruiting Sergeant before them, a man of great experience and expertise at doing so.

"This is not a problem they have in France," declared Ferreira as if in awe of the enemy.

"Because men have no choice, conscription ensures Napoleon has the largest armies in all of Europe, and yet still we knock them down, do you know why?" Craven asked.

"Why?"

"Because a conscripted man is little better than a slave."

"I wouldn't be so sure. Those conscripts have marched across almost all of the continent."

Craven groaned as he knew it were true.

"But surely better to lead free men who chose to take up arms?" Paget asked.

"How free do you think those men are when it requires a handful of lies to make them sign up?" Ferreira asked.

"Come on, we will find no volunteers here." Craven led them on. The recruiting Sergeant giving them a wave as if celebrating his victory upon seeing them off from his turf.

They rode on, passing signs to London and knowing it would be a far shorter trip than heading North to the industrial powerhouse of Manchester, and yet nobody protested as they were all eager to see the home of the Salfords. They continued onwards, with Matthys trying his best to recruit in every town and village on the week-long ride to the city. After spending so much time stuck in Lisbon, it felt good to be on the road again and also to have some freedom away from all the chaos which they had stirred up back in Portugal. They were one day out of Manchester when the Sergeant signed his first recruit.

"It is really not one of his strengths, this recruiting, is it?" Ferreira said quietly beside Paget and Craven.

"We can't all be good at everything," admitted Craven.

"I think Matthys has too much of a conscience for that job. For he is too honest, and few men seem to want to take up this life when they know the realities," replied Paget.

"You did."

"I was sold a different set of lies. For service in the army has been like nothing anyone had prepared me for."

"And you would not have signed up knowing what it would be like?"

"I don't believe I would. Now I would not have missed it for the world, but my younger self would have steered well clear."

"And so perhaps the lies are needed?"

Paget shrugged as he didn't much like the concept, and yet it was hard to disagree considering what he had just admitted to them.

They continued their march with Matthys looking most proud of himself, even having found a small horse for the young man to ride to keep up with them as they made their way North. The next day they made their final approach, but as they drew nearer, the clouds darkened, and the air became thick and foul. They could soon see the smokestacks rising up above the city belching a thick smog into the skies which covered the land for miles around. Ferreira looked impressed and disgusted in equal parts, for he was not at all accustomed to the sight of industrialised towns and cities.

"Is this what the future holds?" he asked almost in despair that his own city might one day look the same. It had not been what he was expecting at all. Paget's descriptions of the vast factories had not prepared him for the smog and strength and intoxication of it all.

"People actually live here?"

"A great many, and in increasing numbers. For the city population has increased more than ten-fold in the past century," replied Matthys.

"Why?" Ferreira was horrified that anyone would choose to come and live in such a hellish landscape after the beautiful countryside they had passed through for several days.

"For work. There is much of it here, and more pay than many could have imagined. Not just for men and women, but for their children, too."

"Hard work it is, back breaking and never ending," replied Moxy seemingly speaking from knowledge.

"But why?"

"To live and to eat."

"I think I'd rather join the army."

"That's what we are counting on," smiled Matthys.

They rolled into the city to find they did not get a fraction of the attention they had elsewhere. It was as if the occupants of the city had become numb to the sight of troops, and not even children playing in the streets looked up at them. It was a bleak city, and yet full of life as busy people went about their lives. Craven led them right to a tavern with plenty of accommodation, but it was little better than a bunkhouse, although nobody protested as he was clearly fond of the place.

"Charming," declared Paget.

"At least it is not on fire," replied Ferreira.

It was a bit soon and still drew some pained smiles from the others. Craven was soon at the bar and settling down for a drink in a place that felt more like home than most. Even so, he had been gone for so long that not a single patron recognised him, not even the barkeep who was unfamiliar to him also.

"What happened to the Fergusons?" he asked after the owners he had known.

"They sold up last year," replied the man who seemed to be the owner, but not much of a conversationalist.

Craven groaned as he had hoped to see some familiar faces.

"Recruiting party?"

"Yes," replied Craven, not bothering to take the time to explain that they were far more than that.

"Good luck to you. You won't find it easy here."

"Why is that?"

"Why would any man march to war to die somewhere in some distant country?"

"It beats dying in this toxic shithole," Ferreira whispered quietly to Gamboa, as both men were starting to regret having left their homeland.

"You hear that, you have your work cut out," said Craven to Matthys, who did not much care for his attitude.

"We will find good strong men here," he insisted.

Craven held up his drink to toast to his success. The days rolled on as Matthys went out each day and struggled to recruit, finding only a single man in three days, and Craven not lifting a finger to help as he gorged himself on food and drink. Matthys returned on the fourth day to find Craven missing from the bar.

"The Captain is across the road," declared Paget.

Matthys groaned as he went out to find him and burst into another tavern. He found Craven sitting at a table playing cards and making merry with many coins committed to the table. Matthys shook his head in disgust.

"Will you join us?" Craven asked jovially.

But Matthys merely walked away, knowing no good would come of making a scene. He committed himself to the task wholeheartedly each day to recruit as best he could. The drinking and gambling continued for days on end as the idle Captain passed the time with every vice he could imagine. Matthys returned to their tavern on the seventh night having another fruitless day and sighed loudly as he sat down.

"No luck?" Paget was enjoying a quiet drink beside Ferreira and Gamboa.

"No, and no thanks to our Captain, for he could be the best asset to this drive to find men," complained Matthys, "And where is the Captain?"

"He left some hours ago with Captains Hawkshaw and

Hunt, for they had an invite to a game."

Matthys was seething as he tried to let it go, but he could not.

"Where?"

"At the Top House," replied Paget.

"The Top House?"

"It is in…" began Paget.

"I know where it is," snarled Matthys, "It is a den of depravity," he whispered.

He shot up from his chair.

"Would you have me escort you?"

"No, save yourself, Lieutenant, I will deal with this."

Ferreira shook his head, knowing no good would come of whatever was about to happen.

"What will the Sergeant do?" Gamboa asked.

"Cause an absolute shit storm to fall upon all our heads, I am sure."

"Perhaps he is right to do so?" Gamboa said. They were all feeling abandoned by Craven, as they had lost their purpose.

"Did you really just say that?" Ferreira asked.

"We came here to recruit and to see the origins of the Salfords, but what have we done? What has Craven done? He is a war hero who could rally men to this regiment, and instead, he sits idly by and lets Matthys struggle on."

"I would keep those opinions to yourself."

"Then you will do nothing either?"

"What would you have me do? I can't change Craven. He is what he is."

But Gamboa was not convinced, and he watched Matthys storm out of the tavern to go and find the Captain in what they all knew would be a fiery encounter, the likes of which none of them wanted to get in the way of. Paget got up to follow him, but Charlie grabbed his arm and held him in place.

"Don't do it, nothing good can come of it," she insisted.

Paget felt completely out of place in the Northern industrial metropolis. It was even more alien to him than the foreign countries they had fought across. He relaxed, taking her advice. Despite all they had been through, he was aware she still knew the Captain better.

* * *

A cheer rang out as Craven won a game, and he celebrated as if it was one of many, but in truth it was the first in a while.

"More wine!" Hunt cried out in honour of his victory.

"I think you've had quite enough already," replied Hawkshaw who was by far the most sober and sensible of them all.

"Nonsense!" Hunt leant against the table where the game was being played, but his hand slipped, and he collapsed onto the edge of the table. It toppled under his weight as everything on it was cast into the air. Playing cards and wine was thrown in all directions as those at the table recoiled in shock and anger. Hunt collapsed to the floor with an immense crash. He slurred his words as he tried to get back up but could not even lift his own bodyweight.

"Come on, what is this!" demanded one of the players angrily as Craven and Hawkshaw helped the drunken fool to his feet. Though in truth Craven was not far behind him. He already felt unsteady and uncoordinated as he beat the accusing man's hand out of the way.

"Our friend here has had a little too much fun, and do not tell me we are not all a little guilty of that sometimes!" Craven said, trying to calm their nerves.

The angry players groaned in agreement. They could all think of times when they had humiliated themselves before their peers, and so they turned their attention back to table as they tried to reconstitute it as best as possible.

"I can stand just fine," complained Hunt. He pushed his way out of their grasp only to stagger back and have to be caught.

"Your evening is done," declared Craven.

He did not argue any further, as he knew protesting was futile. He also knew they were right, for he was ruined.

"We are all not long for bed," replied Hawkshaw.

"Can you get him back?"

"You are not coming?" he asked his brother.

"I just won a game. My luck finally turned, and so it's no time to stop now," smiled Craven.

Hawkshaw did not look convinced, but he was too tired to argue about it.

"Come on, let's get you home."

Hawkshaw wrapped one of Hunt's arms over his shoulder and helped him to the door. They staggered a few yards outside when Craven heard Hunt vomiting violently. He smiled. It was not his problem, and he was thankful they had made it to the street. He watched with glee as the gambling table was prepared for another game and more wine was brought for him. He knew if he drank much more he would soon follow in the steps of

Archie Hunt, but he didn't much care. He was now safe in England and couldn't imagine anything awful happening to him, beyond collapsing drunk in the gutter. And that was an experience he was well accustomed to and could live with the consequences that would mostly just be shame, for which he did not care, nor could he be made to feel embarrassed. He went on playing, but he had soon spent all he had, and yet he was not even mad, having enjoyed himself greatly. He slammed his hands down on the table and rose up on to his feet, swaying a little from side to side. He was not as bad as Hunt, but he was certainly catching him up.

"I bid you a goodnight, gentlemen!"

They cheered in support, having not only enjoyed his company but also their pockets he had lined with his money.

"I'll be off."

Craven he swayed a little more before finding his balance. He walked out into the street to be met with the foul stench of Archie's vomit, but it was at least enough of a shock to his senses to sober him up a little, along with a light breeze which was welcome against his sweaty face. His cheeks were flushed red from his excesses.

"Craven!" A man in shadow suddenly stormed towards him.

"Yes?" Craven smiled.

It was Matthys who stepped out into the light, taking one look at his drunken state before giving the most disapproving look of disgust.

"I don't have the energy for one of your lectures," groaned Craven.

"Can you not remain sober for just a few days?"

"Not whilst there is something to drink, and I have the monies to pay for it!" Craven laughing greatly as if finding himself hilariously funny.

"And do you have money?"

Craven reached for his coin purse and held it up to see that it was feather light and completely empty.

"No, but tomorrow is a new day!"

Matthys looked appalled.

"Christ save me, for you are less of a handful when there is a war to fight."

The sound of horse hooves echoed out louder every second as they approached, an unusual sight so late at night. Matthys pulled Craven back to the edge of the street as three riders approached, but instead of riding past they came to a halt and approached. As they came into the candlelight, Matthys recognised the man leading them immediately, for it was Timmerman. He pushed Craven back against the wall behind them, for which he could not resist and crashed back into it. Matthys drew out his sword in readiness to defend himself and Craven.

"What do you want?" he demanded.

"You know what I want," replied Timmerman slyly.

"Can a man not be left in peace?" Craven pleaded.

"Peace? There will be no peace. Where is Hawkshaw? Where is your brother?" Timmerman snarled.

Craven shrugged as if pretending to have no idea, but that angered Timmerman, and he climbed down from his horse. He handed the reins to one of his men and drew out his sword. He advanced towards them but stopped three yards short, well out of striking distance, leaving his sword hanging menacingly down by his side as a less than subtle threat. Matthys raised his own sword.

"We aren't here to fight, but we will not hesitate to defend ourselves!" Matthys shouted at him.

But Timmerman just glared back at them as if awaiting his answer.

"We are in England now, not the frontier," protested Matthys at the prospect of an attack.

"I couldn't care if we were on hallowed ground or the steps of Horse Guards, I demand satisfaction. And if you will not tell me where I can find it, then I will end you here as an appetizer, and then find Hawkshaw and finish him, too!"

"We will never give up one of our own!"

Matthys meant it, and no matter how angry he was with Craven, he would risk his life to defend him.

"Tell me where I can find that worm Hawkshaw or die!"

"You would kill us over this?" Matthys asked in disgust.

"I have killed for far less, and you mean nothing to me," replied Timmerman as he waited for Matthys' decision.

"I will never give up a friend, not for any price."

Timmerman groaned before storming forward. He struck against Matthys' sword, beating it one way and then engaging against it to drive a thrust towards his heart, as if to do what he had promised and end them there and then. Matthys parried off the blow, but Timmerman kept coming forwards and slammed his ward iron into the Sergeant's head. It knocked him unconscious, and he watched with glee as he collapsed onto the street. Matthys was a good fighter, but completely out of Timmerman's league, and it showed. And yet he had held his ground for what he believed in, although that meant nothing to the sadistic Timmerman who thought only of himself.

It was another sobering moment for Craven who found his second wind. He managed to stand upright long enough to draw out his sword and hold it in guard.

"Look at you, a ruin of a man who ran back to England to flee his troubles. A hero they call you, but what kind of hero flees from the war?"

Craven could find no words to explain it, as he could not help but feel there was some truth to it.

"You are every bit the coward Colonel Bevan was, a disgrace to the army and to this country."

Craven hated what he was hearing, but he knew he was in no condition to fight and so made no attempt to aggravate the situation any further.

"I demand you tell me where Hawkshaw is, and I will spare your cowardly life."

Craven shook his head. For if there was one thing he shared in common with Matthys, it was his unwavering support and loyalty to his comrades.

"So be it."

Timmerman stormed forward. He engaged against Craven's blade just as he had the Sergeant's, but even in his drunken form, Craven was a more dangerous and nimble opponent. He parried several blows, but Timmerman kept going forward. Craven moved into the street to get some space. He did not have the stability or strength to go to grappling. Timmerman was faster moving forward and beat his blade, closing in for the same brutal punch with his ward iron as he had given Matthys. Craven narrowly ducked out of the way and smiled at his success, only to find Timmerman's clenched left fist follow and crack him on the temple. Craven staggered back several paces. His legs were weak, and his balance was thrown off. The adrenaline pumping through his body countered some of the effects of the wine, but he was in a bad way, and Timmerman just kept coming. He gave ground as he parried more blows and spun out from one huge cut. He crashed into another wall and ducked, just in time to miss a sabre slash that crashed into the wall where his head had been.

Timmerman was throwing deadly blows without any restraint at all. Craven could see openings as his old adversary was wild and letting his anger fuel exaggerated movements. Even though Craven could identify the openings, he was too slow and weak to take advantage of them. He rushed on down the street to gain more distance. With every step he took, he was beginning to sober up, and yet he could barely move in a straight line after the blow to the temple. Timmerman gave pursuit with murderous intent as his rage had been stewing for months. In his eyes Craven was now just as bad as Hawkshaw, and their old rivalry was rekindled. Craven parried blow after blow without his usual precision but doing enough to protect himself, and yet many of Timmerman's blows were passing worryingly close to his body as he struggled to get to each parry in time.

"Stop there!" a voice shouted out.

Two watchmen raced onto the scene from a side street to intervene and directed their staffs at the two swordsmen. Timmerman merely grabbed one of the staffs and ripped it from the watchman's hand, tossing it aside to a look of horror from the man.

"I am Major Timmerman. Think about that before you make another move!"

Two more of the watchmen joined their comrades, but they heard the statement and looked at one another in horror. For they were quite accustomed to dealing with drunken enlisted soldiers and sailors, but never an officer, and certainly not one of such a high rank.

"Walk away," growled Timmerman.

His words carried weight, and they soon turned their backs, washing their hands of whatever it was they had witnessed.

Craven was panting but had managed to catch a few breaths as Timmerman looked on at him with a smirk, seemingly holding all of the power. He raced on after Craven who parried blows one after the other. He even returned a few as he ran on in hope of lasting long enough to sober up further to put up a decent contest; especially as it was his life he now gambled with. But as he stepped into a crossroads, he heard the gallop of horses and could see Timmerman's men advance to close off his path to safety. He came to a halt, gasping for breath, and accepting he could go no further. He was wide awake now but still weak and clumsy. His balance was shot and every move he made wild. He circled Timmerman casually in a moment of calm.

"I should have killed you years ago, but better late than never. I will run my sword through your heart and then find your brother for a double bill," smirked Timmerman.

Craven did not rise to aggression and continued on calmly. He suddenly lashed out to hit Timmerman before he could lift his guard. It was a noble effort, but he was not nearly fast enough, and his old enemy parried with his sword, driving a fist into his gut. The wind was taken out of Craven as he staggered back and folded over, barely staying on his feet. He was kicking himself. He had taken far worse blows as a stage gladiator and shrugged them off to keep up the fight. He was weak and exhausted with seemingly nowhere to run or hide, and the one thing he had relied on, the sword, to get him out of the worst of trouble was not going to cut it this time. He smiled at the absurdity of the situation as he wasn't going to die in a bad mood.

"Last chance, Craven. Tell me where I can find Hawkshaw, and all of this will be over."

Craven spat on the ground before them. Timmerman lifted his sword to make his final pass at Craven, but a booming voice rang out.

"Put your sword down!" the stranger roared.

It made Timmerman pause and look for the source, just in time to see a man approaching through the shadows and finally into the light. At which point Timmerman got a glance at the man's silver hair and seemingly frail-looking face.

"Mathewson?" Craven asked in amazement.

"Leave us, old man!" Timmerman sneered at him.

"I will not," replied the old man, in a well-educated Scottish accent.

"I am Major…" began Timmerman.

But he was cut short by Mathewson.

"I don't care who you are. You have no business here!"

Timmerman approached him in an attempt to intimidate, but Mathewson lifted his arm slightly from where it had been dangling and concealing the sword he had in hand down the length of his body. It was a Highland basket hilt broadsword, not of the regimental types carried by Highland officers in the service now, but of a more elaborate form as carried by the Highlanders in their daily lives since before the Jacobite uprising. It had a robust and highly elaborate basket hilt guard which extended far over the wrist in a way that no other sword did and featured a long and broad double-edged blade. Timmerman stopped, surprised to see such a weapon, but he then he smiled.

"Come on, old man, you should have long since hung up your sword."

"And you should have learnt some manners by your age."

Timmerman looked back at Craven, growing impatient as the first of his targets was within his grasp now.

"Don't make me hurt you, old man," he sighed, lifting his sword up to threaten Mathewson, but he was stunned by the old man's quick reactions.

He lifted the broadsword up and dealt a very fast beat, the speed and weight of the blade carrying Timmerman's blade far out of line. He looked stunned, but quickly recovered it, and directed it forward again. But Mathewson came forward, engaging Timmerman's blade and forcing him to apply pressure against it, as he backed away to maintain distance.

Timmerman did not know how to react to his aggressive footwork and launched a quick cut around the broadsword, but Mathewson parried it and returned the same blow with twice as much strength. Timmerman tried two again, only for the old man to reply in the same way as if to mock him in mimicking his actions. Timmerman smiled, realising he could use it against Mathewson, and this time after he attacked, he timed Mathewson's motions, expecting to put him at the mercy of his sabre. But Mathewson reacted so calmly it was as if he had already known what was coming, and he struck the sabre with a short beat of the back edge of his broadsword. Mathewson was both strong and precise in every one of his actions, and this was no exception. Timmerman's blade was cast aside, and the Major found a broadsword blade within an inch of his throat.

Timmerman back away in surprise, and not wanting anything more to do with the old man as he looked to Craven, realising he was now more hassle than he was worth.

"I will find Hawkshaw, and when I do, he is a dead man!"

Craven nodded in agreement as he merely wanted it all to be over, for he was exhausted.

"Come on, I have wasted enough time on these fools!"

Timmerman walked away to the horse his men had led for him. He mounted up and glared at Craven once more before turning and leaving them be.

"Thanks," he gasped in relief.

"I see trouble still follows you," replied Mathewson.

"I wish I could say this one was my fault, but that bastard wants my brother."

"Brother?"

"Yes, I was as surprised as you."

"Will you retire to my home for a dram?"

"I'd love to, but I left a man behind, and that will not do."

Mathewson appreciated the sentiment.

"I hear you have made quite a name for yourself in Portugal."

"For better and worse," admitted Craven.

"Tomorrow at noon the local militias will be gathered for exercises. Come and see as my guest, and any who ride with you."

"You are still at it, then?"

"Until I can no longer breathe or lift a sword."

Craven smiled in agreement.

"Good night and thank you."

He sheathed his sword and ran on to find Matthys. The old grey-haired swordsman shook his head and smiled. For such a reunion with an old friend would have been a surprise if it were anyone else, but for Craven it was no surprise at all.

CHAPTER 13

Craven awoke and got up, his head a little sore and his memory vague, but it was starting to return. He went downstairs to find his friends awaiting him. Matthys was sitting up on a bench, looking worse for wear. They were all there but Hawkshaw and Hunt, which was cause for concern, as he began to wonder if they had made it back the night before.

"Where is my brother?" Craven demanded as most of then sat idly about enjoying some breakfast without any cares in the world.

"Here," replied Hawkshaw as he raced past with a bowl of food in hand.

Craven breathed a sigh of relief.

"The Sergeant tells me you encountered some trouble last night?"

"You could say that."

"Another bar fight, was it?"

Hawkshaw appeared oblivious to the facts and danger to them. He looked to Matthys in surprise as to why he had not explained any of it, and yet there was a vagueness in his eyes. He clearly didn't remember much of the night, and so he was the only one who knew of Timmerman's return. He looked around at his comrades and could not bring himself to tell them and sour the mood. He convinced himself that it was not a problem, and that in a sober state and amongst friends there was no danger.

"We met with a little trouble."

"Who struck me on the head?" Matthys asked.

Craven shrugged, for he did not want to lie.

"I met an old friend last night, and he has invited us to public militia training exercises later this morning," he declared, adeptly changing the subject and thought ahead to better times. He knew they would have to face the scourge that was Timmerman again, but he put the Major to the back of his mind, for he would cross that bridge when he reached it. Deep down he knew it was a mistake, but they all needed a lift to their spirits, and he had the chance now.

"What old friend?" Matthys asked who seemed to have recovered a little.

"Mathewson," smiled Craven.

"Thomas Mathewson, really?"

"That old bastard is still alive?" Birback asked.

"Alive and as strong as ever it seemed to me."

"Are we to watch a great show, Sir?" Paget asked excitedly.

"Watch? I think Mathewson would have those men tested against us."

"Truly, Sir?"

"Any excuse for a little sword training and contest."

It was not long before they were on their way, walking through the busy streets of Manchester as a rabble. The people of the city gave them no time nor space, shoving past them with no respect for the uniforms they wore. For they had become numb to them, and even the officers were nudged out of the way by passing labourers. Ferreira had almost been thrown onto his back by one burly man.

"What a God-awful place," he declared as they went on.

After the beauty of the Portuguese landscape, it was no surprise the city was an awful experience in their eyes. Ferreira already longed for the sea once more, for he had so often lived near it in all his years, and to be so intoxicated by the fumes of the industrial centre was stifling.

"Who is Thomas Mathewson?" Paget asked Matthys, knowing he was the one who would know best and be most willing to share what he knew.

"A great swordsman, but more than that, a great teacher of the sword."

"Captain's Craven's teacher?"

"One of them certainly."

Paget was bubbling with excitement to meet the teacher behind Craven's greatness and gained quite the spring in his step. It was not long before they passed the spot where Matthys and Craven had been attacked. Craven noticed it sparked some memories for the Sergeant and that he was concerned, yet he shook his head as a complete picture of the evening's events still alluded him.

"Is everything okay?" Paget asked him.

"This is where I was attacked, but I can only wonder why,

for I have no quarrels with any man in England."

Paget could believe it.

"A ruffian? A thief? Perhaps someone after your belongings."

"And yet they got nothing."

"Probably because Craven saw them off. Whoever your attackers were, you were lucky he found you."

Matthys groaned as he knew there would be so much more to the story, if only he could remember what had happened. The sound of a musket volley rang out in the distance, and it made him jump a little. It was the last thing he expected to hear so far from the war, but he kicked himself for such a reaction. He should know better, having loosed off many hundreds if not thousands of musket shots whilst in the service of the Manchester and Salford Independent Rifle Regiment. It seemed like a lifetime ago. They went on to find a large public park where soldiers carried out all manner of exercises as the public gathered about to watch the spectacle. Yeomanry cavalry galloped about the fields as if they thundered towards French lines, conducting themselves with much pomp.

"Magnificent!" Paget stopped in amazement.

Craven shook his head as he couldn't understand how the display could impress a man who had lived through such large-scale battles under the command of Wellington himself, and Paget was easily pleased. Horse drawn artillery conducted manoeuvres in the distance as they practiced quickly limbering and unlimbering their guns and moving whilst conducting firing drills. Hundreds of infantrymen marched back and forth, conducting complex unit drills that many regular soldiers would never be capable of.

"Quite the circus, isn't it?" Hunt didn't mean it kindly.

"It is not something to be ridiculed, for these men train hard and well and will be the backbone of England should the French ever attempt an invasion," replied Paget in their defence.

Hunt laughed.

"You think these toy soldiers could stop the French? They are shopkeepers and bankers putting on a costume to please children and baying crowds," replied Hunt disparagingly.

"Captain Craven was one of them, was he not? Many of those who now march with us would have been out here doing the same only a few years ago. Men who have seen far more of war than you. Or do you think Craven only plays at war?"

"I think Mr Paget rather has you by the balls," chuckled Craven.

Hunt looked stunned, but he took it in good spirits and laughed in response. The group's attention was soon drawn to a party of several dozen soldiers. They took up positions close to a crowd with single sticks in hand under the supervision of Mathewson. He carried his broadsword in hand but still wore no uniform. He placed them in lines and began shouting his words of command, taking them through the paces of partnered drills. They were clearly well practiced, and not a single mistake as attacks and parries were made in perfect harmony.

"That is your old teacher, Sir?" Paget asked.

"It is, Mr Thomas Mathewson. An old soldier with much to say about the sword, and he will eagerly explain to all who will listen how the broadsword is superior to all other weapons."

"It is, Sir?" asked Paget in surprise.

"No, but you have to respect his passion," smiled Craven.

They watched along with the crowd as the soldiers went

through a series of drills, not just by command but from memory. It was an impressive display of both physical and mental training and fortitude, but soon enough they split off and began to fight another with their singlesticks in free play. Paget smiled as it was strongly reminiscent of the training he had regularly practiced ever since meeting Captain Craven. It reminded him of their first encounter when he experienced the singlestick, having only ever used foils. With two years of training, he now felt so comfortable with them it was as if he was born to them, but the humbling experience of his first time always weighed on his mind on such an occasion.

The volunteer and militia soldiers gave a spirited display and soon caught the attention of Craven. He could not stay away and led them on to get a closer look. Mathewson lit up upon catching a glimpse of him, and Paget could tell there was a deep and longing connection between the two men. He found it fascinating. He had never met anyone from Craven's past, except perhaps Timmerman, and that was far from a positive experience.

"The Salford Slayer returns!" Mathewson called out.

"That was what they called you, Sir? Surely not."

"No, they really did not," he smiled.

Craven embraced his old master with a great hug as though no time had passed at all.

"I thought when the Salfords came to an end, you would surely call it a day and retire somewhere quiet and give all this up," said Craven.

"Nonsense! What sort of life is that for a man of action!"

Craven couldn't help but agree, as he could never imagine himself retiring to the quiet life either.

"No, not whilst I can stand and hold my broadsword, and especially not when there are men who need to be trained now more so than ever!"

"But they will not go to war," questioned Craven, who looked down upon them as toy soldiers who would never leave the country and face the French in battle.

"You did, James, you did."

Craven was stunned and could not argue with his point.

"So, will you put these fine young men to the test?"

"You would have me fight them?" Craven sounded as if it were beneath him.

"You were once a gladiator, James, and you took on all comers, has that changed?" Craven smiled as the old fencing master knew just how to get under his skin, "And how about your men? Will they rise to the challenge?" Mathewson pressed.

"I'd love to!" Paget answered before Craven could get in a word.

Craven shook his head. He was in no state for it, and yet the peer pressure was immense. Many of the fighters had even stopped to await his response, but Mathewson did not wait for it as he addressed the crowd.

"Look at this! One of our very own and a hero of the Peninsula campaign, Captain James Craven!"

They roared with excitement as they all seemingly knew of his exploits.

"You hear that, James? They all want to be you. I told them you are one of the best there is, so do not disappoint them," smiled Mathewson proudly.

Craven took a deep breath and exhaled, realising it was going to be a long day. He began to take off his sword belt and jacket to a cheer from the fighters who knew they were going to get their crack at the infamous Captain Craven. And yet he did not have the look of a fresh man arriving to the field after a good night's rest.

"You don't have to do this," Ferreira declared, who looked even less enthusiastic for the prospect of heavy exercises and enthusiastic young men trying to bash their heads in. Though the truth was they were not all so young, as the volunteer regiments attracted all sorts. In the distance they could see the militia going through regimental exercises, and they looked competent but not half as eager and confident as the volunteers Mathewson had taught.

"Yes, he does."

"Ferreira looked astonished as he awaited an explanation from Paget.

"The Captain has a reputation to keep. A reputation which is vital to recruiting, and to the morale of those who follow him, let alone the effects it has on the French."

"Has that not been well earned by now?"

"People are quick to forget, and many would gleefully see Captain Craven fall from grace, just as we saw it happen back in Lisbon."

Ferreira groaned, accepting there was some truth to it, but Paget continued on pressing his points.

"What would people say if the great swordsman that is Captain Craven turned down a fight? And in front of an audience, no less? When you build a reputation as a fighter, you have to keep on fighting."

"Yes, yes, I've heard enough!"

Craven had already accepted his fate. As he gave his

equipment to them, he noticed Amyn watching the martial display with great intrigue. He had played with singlesticks with Craven and the others many times but had never seen others do so, and especially not on such a grand scale.

"Something interesting?"

"It reminds me of home," he replied as he looked out at the displays of skill being conducted by riders in the distance, and the crowd roaring with excitement with every jump and blow that was struck. Cavalrymen hacked down against melons balanced on poles whilst others conducted more wild feats. One rider rode with a sabre in each hand and cut with both simultaneously at the gallop, which greatly delighted the crowds.

"Join us, then," insisted Craven.

"You would permit it?" Amyn looked to Mathewson.

"You will stand on your own merit here. To the roar of the crowd upon your victories and to their laughter at your expense if you are not up to the task."

Craven smirked, knowing well enough the Mamluk's skills, but Amyn remained stoic. He bowed his head a little in respect and appreciation for the seemingly great honour of being permitted to take part in such a grand exercise. Though Craven knew the Mamluk swordsman also had no notion of being laughed at, for he knew his own skills and now understood the European methods well enough to contend against them better than ever before.

"Would you honour us with a bout upon the scaffold?" Mathewson asked Craven.

Craven nodded in agreement as he looked out at the raised wooden platform, which was commonly assembled for great contests and drew much of the audience's eye for its prominent position. Two men slugged it out with their bare fists to the roar of the crowd, but as Craven watched, he saw one deliver a crippling hook to the liver of his opponent. The man doubled over and crashed to the hard scaffold deck, reeling in pain. The audience roared with delight as the other bloody man threw up his hands in celebration.

"You English seem to make war where there is none," declared Vicenta.

"And you do not? I have lived through your training days."

"Gruelling, yes, but we do not destroy one another," she replied.

"And what would you know of fighting?" Mathewson asked the Spanish woman, as if insulted she would question their ways.

"A great deal," smiled Craven.

Mathewson looked stunned, but he shrugged it off as though he had not heard, an ignorance which made Craven smile further.

"Nooth!" Mathewson roared.

The fighters came to an immediate halt as their fencing Master called for his man and nodded towards the scaffold. The man who climbed onto the platform did not look like much. He was of average stature and could not be any older than Paget. Craven tore off his shirt, revealing a score of old scars. He strode forward, took a singlestick from a rack, and raced to take up position upon the deck.

"Who is that?" a stranger asked from behind Paget.

"Captain James Craven," replied the Lieutenant proudly.

He heard whispers behind him as the news rapidly spread

through the rest of the people. His arrival had not been announced, but soon most of the crowd knew it was him before the fight had even begun, and all eyes were fixed on the Captain. He took up position on the square scaffold which was only thirty feet long and with no barriers, so that if you went off the edge you would plunge almost ten feet to the ground below. Hay had been scattered to give some little relief to those who took the unfortunate tumble where their egos would be bruised even more than their bodies under the roar and laughter of the crowd.

"Mr Craven, it is an honour to fight you," declared Nooth.

Craven looked appreciative, but continued before he could get a word in.

"It would be a privilege to defeat you."

Craven smiled at the tenacity and confidence of the young man.

"Have you ever gone to war?"

"No, but whilst you were away, we all kept on getting better. But you are a scarred old man."

Craven was curious now as to his opponent's level. He had supreme confidence and did not even seem to mean offence by his statements, more saying it in a matter-of-fact way, speaking simply and honestly as Ellis did.

"Old?" Craven whispered to himself.

He had always thought of himself as a dashing young fellow. Yet it was true that amongst the Nooths and Pagets of the world he was indeed old, and his body certainly felt it at times. In that regard, Nooth was also correct. He had been through the wars and was often reminded of it when he tried to get up out of bed on a cold morning. Though he wondered how much the wars had played in that part and how much of it had been the battering he had endured as a stage gladiator. Either way, he was not a young man anymore, and yet with his years of hardship and suffering had come a lot of experience and knowledge.

He saluted his opponent who returned the gesture. There were no judges nor even a referee as those on stage fought until their opponent was defeated. Both men knew what that meant. Victory could be achieved by forcing your opponent to fall from the scaffold, by causing a cut more than an inch on the head, or by them being unable to continue, voluntarily or not. It was a brutal affair which Craven thrived in and had come to love many years ago.

Both fighters came to their guards as the audience watched on in complete silence and with great anticipation to see what it would be like to witness Captain Craven fight before their very eyes. He was as still as a statue as Nooth crept cautiously forward into the danger zone. That was the distance at which either man could strike the other with a single lunge, or extension of the front foot and bending of the body forward. Nooth probed with light cuts to either side of Craven's singlestick, but he did not respond. He held his stick out in front, dividing his body in two and relying on the leather basket guard to protect his hand and arm in such a way as he could not depend on his fighting swords to.

It could be considered poor form or even cheating if they were trying to exactly replicate a real fight, but this was anything but. It was a sporting endeavour where each man would try to win in any way he could within the rules. Nooth smiled at Craven's composure as he did not even flinch, an attribute one only saw in two types of fighters; beginners too slow to respond, or even knew they needed to respond, and those so highly advanced they had complete confidence in their own timing and distance.

Nooth would not have expected anything less, but he was right to be cautious. For the third time he tried to probe at Craven's defences, and he was met with a lashing response from the Captain who threw towards his head with a strong blow. Nooth parried it and tried to respond with a fast riposte, but Craven parried it quickly and responded with an even more powerful counter once again to the man's head. Nooth's singlestick shook violently upon the parry, which caused him to stagger back a little in surprise at the blow and how much power had been generated in such a short time.

Craven smiled at his opponent's response, but Nooth did the same. He was merely getting warmed up to his new opponent and what he had to offer. He came forward again and probed Craven's defences, throwing quickly at his legs. Such a blow would not end the fight, but it would certainly slow a fighter down. Craven slipped his leg back to avoid the blow and was mostly successful, but he still felt the very tip of the singlestick tap his thigh. It was not enough to be considered a blow and went unnoticed to the crowd, but not to Craven, who knew it came too close for comfort. Nooth could sense it, too, and he pressed on.

He attacked with repeated quick blows that put Craven on the back foot, as he edged closer to the edge and felt his heel balance over the edge, to the gasp of the crowd. He ducked under an over enthusiastic swing from Nooth who thought to have a theatrical finish to their encounter. Craven steadied his footing in the centre of the platform and took up his guard once again, but Nooth had gained massively in confidence, believing he was in complete control of the fight.

"Come on, Sir!" Paget shouted in support, desperate to see his Captain succeed before the large number of people.

Craven took it more seriously now as he could see a major threat was before him. He needed to get on the offensive and give Nooth something more to think and to worry about. He pressed forward and engaged the two sticks, rotating and driving a sneaky thrust over the top of Nooth's guard, but it was merely a deception. Craven lashed a cut over onto the other side of his stick. Nooth got to the parry at the last moment, and although he took most of the energy out of the strike, he could not stop the stick smacking him in the forehead. The blow was reduced to a light tap, but it was enough to cause concern. He'd come close to taking a crushing blow to the skull which would often render a man unconscious and spell defeat, both in battle and in this contest. Nooth recognised the same danger Craven had seen and also upped the tempo. The two sticks clashed time and time again in a fine display of skill that provided plenty of entertainment to those watching.

"James is slipping. He would have finished this by now just a few years ago," declared Mathewson.

"He toys with your man and plays to the crowd." Paget quickly came to the defence of his Captain, but he shot a concerned glance to Ferreira and whispered to him, "He is, isn't he?"

Ferreira shrugged as he had no idea, and that concerned Paget who tried his utmost to hide his fears.

Craven and Nooth continued to strike at one another with both speed and grace, but Craven was breathing heavily and beginning to slow down. His movements became less refined, and his cuts swung more wildly. Nooth seized his opportunity and launched another prolonged attack, again swinging for Craven's leg. This time he could not get out of the way, and the heavy ash stave crashed into his thigh. Craven winced in pain as his leg buckled a little, but he recoiled quickly and stormed at Nooth, knowing that despite his fading energy he still had strength on his side.

He crashed into the man and drove him several paces back, smashing the basket of his singlestick into the young man's head with a brutal punch, launching him over the edge of the scaffold. It sent him crashing down onto the hay below, and he rolled out onto the grass. The crowd cheered at the display that had hardly been conducted under the rules with which such a contest would normally be done, but nobody complained; not even Nooth who would not stoop so low as to protest, for he had too much pride. Craven threw up his hand triumphantly, but he looked exhausted as he stepped off the stage and tossed the stick away and then retired to his comrades.

"Well done, Sir!" Paget roared.

"Service abroad has made you weak," declared Mathewson.

Craven nodded along, not wanting to admit the hard partying and drinking was more to blame.

He looked over Paget's shoulder to see a pickpocket lifting the Lieutenant's purse.

"Leave it be!"

Paget looked surprised as he turned around to see the young man trying to steal from him.

"Damn you, Sir, damn you for your impudence that you

would steal from a man in uniform!" he roared incredulously.

The thief froze, knowing he had been caught outright, and he looked either side to see redcoats all around.

"Sorry, Sir."

"No, you're not, but nice try," Craven added.

"No, I'm not," he smiled.

"What's your name?"

"People call me Quicks."

"Because you have quick fingers?"

"That's right."

"You might be quick with your fingers, but you are not so quick with your head. You would do wise to choose your targets more carefully. Go on, get out of here."

"You will let this criminal go?"

"I was once that criminal," Craven smiled back at Paget.

The young man fled and joined several other young men who were clearly up to the same mischief.

"What lesson did you teach him, Sir? By letting him off from his crimes?"

"That he should not get caught, for most would not let him off."

Paget looked disgusted and also a bit confused that Craven would be so flippant. A cheer roared from the crowd, and they turned back. Amyn was standing alone on the scaffold whilst his vanquished opponent staggered to his feet on the ground below, having been defeated in a matter of seconds.

"Your foreign fellow puts on far better a showing of himself!" Mathewson concluded.

Craven was still panting from the exertion. It had taken far more out of him than it should have, but he smiled as they laughed together. Drums beat in the distance, and cavalry squadrons raced onto the field. Several formations formed up in battle lines for a grand display as a mock battle erupted before their eyes. It was a great display of pageantry and a fantastical spectacle, the perfect battle, something that never existed on the real battlefield, both sides playing their part exactly as intended. Yet the cloud of powder smoke and the putrid smell of sulphur was every bit as real as the battlefields of Portugal and Spain, and oddly made Craven feel a sense of homesickness. It was much the same feeling he had experienced upon seeing England for the first time in two years, and yet now he missed Portugal. But it was more than that. He missed the military life and the war. It was an uneasy and bizarre feeling, as he was reminded of the man he was when he had left England. He avoided war and military exercises like the plague, and yet he had somehow grown so fond of them he felt out of sorts being so many thousands of miles away.

With this new sensation, Craven watched the mock battle with great intrigue and enthusiasm, as if he had stepped into Paget's shoes, for his eyes lit up with a youthful enthusiasm.

CHAPTER 14

Beer tankards crashed together as the men of the Salfords made merry with the militia officers and volunteers at an inn at the edge of the field where the great mock battle had entertained the crowds. Many of which had flocked to the same watering hole to chat with the soldiers as if they were the same heroes who had returned from Portugal and Spain. Paget looked around in surprise to see that few came to talk with the real soldiers who had fought in the war.

"Is this what it was like for you and the Captain, Sir? Playing at war?" Paget asked Matthys.

The Sergeant smiled and nodded in agreement.

"They were fine times indeed, or at least when Craven wasn't getting himself and the rest of us into trouble," he admitted.

"But they talk as if the war was here and they were living and experiencing it," Paget sounded both insulted and confused in equal measure.

"You must remember, Lieutenant, that the threat of England's invasion by Bonaparte was a very real possibility not so long ago, and it could be again. For that is the way the world turns. These men might not have ever fought in a battle, but they stepped up to defend their country the same as you did. They readied themselves to defend England's shores, and they continue to do so. You were once just like them. You put on a uniform and practiced and played at war well before having ever seen it. Many soldiers go their entire lives without ever seeing a battle. We should all be so lucky, but we do not live in those times. We live in the days of a great war not seen since more than a century and a half."

Paget calmed a little as Matthys' explanation was both fair and reasonable, and Paget was one of the few men the Sergeant knew he could reason with. The young man was ever enthusiastic to learn in any way he could, an unusual trait amongst all men. Paget looked across to where Craven had been sitting on the opposite side of the table as Mathewson arrived with a fresh drink for the Captain, but he was nowhere to be seen.

"Outside," declared Matthys who had been most observant even during conversation.

Mathewson took the beers outside where he found Craven alone and deep in thought, with only the faint ambient light of a lantern hanging by the door lighting the side of his face. Craven didn't even seem to notice his arrival until the tankard was thrust into his hands.

"Thank you," he replied in surprise.

"What is on your mind?"

Craven said nothing as if pretending it was nothing,

"Come on, James, I've never known you to spend this long thinking about anything. You act or you forget and move on, and so what can now weigh so heavily on those shoulders? You're not still fretting about the contest earlier today? Worried that you came close to defeat?"

"I did not," he snapped.

But Mathewson smirked, for they both knew he was lucky to come out on top. He had only done so through brute strength and not skill, which was the sign of a poor swordsman.

"Come on, James, what is it?"

Mathewson pressed on in genuine concern as though he spoke to a close family member. They had not seen one another for several years, but for all of Mathewson's jabs at his expense, it was clear he cared greatly for his former prodigy. Craven took a deep breath and sighed, readying to reveal his woes of which he didn't feel so comfortable in sharing.

"Captain Hawkshaw."

"Yes?"

"He is my brother, by blood."

"And this is a problem?"

"Yes, in a way. The man who came to take my life is really after my brother. Or I suppose both of us, but his grievance is chiefly with Hawkshaw."

"And it is a justified grievance?"

"It is," smiled Craven, and he could not help but laugh, as he could not imagine how the circumstances could be any worse.

Mathewson sipped on his drink and said nothing, which frustrated Craven as he awaited a response.

"Well, what should I do?"

"Sometimes you must let men settle things for themselves, and by stepping between them, you only delay the inevitable and put more at stake."

Craven groaned in agreement, but the more he thought about it, the more it made sense. He thought back to all the encounters he had settled by fighting and wondered why his brother should be any different. It felt as though a great weight had been lifted from his shoulders. He held up his tankard in salute as appreciation for his old master's wisdom. They clashed the two together and went on drinking, heading back inside to join the others where they found Paget eagerly awaiting his arrival.

"Are you okay, Sir?"

"Of course," replied Craven confidently. He was not even pretending now, for he felt so much better about the mess they had found themselves in.

"I suppose you came to England to recruit?" Mathewson asked.

"We certainly did," replied Paget.

"And yet you came here to attempt to rob us of our local lads who may yet receive my instruction?"

He sounded a little angry but also playful.

"It can't be any worse than down South. Recruiting is no easy game," replied Craven.

"Not even with your name and fame?"

"A few students of fencing might know my name, but I am hardly famous," he grumbled.

A particularly rowdy mob of soldiers drew their attention, whose ringleader was Nooth. He was regaling them with his exploits of fighting with Craven as if he had been the winner of their contest.

"Excuse me, gentlemen, but my work is not done. Good luck in your endeavours and hopefully we shall meet again before you depart for Portugal once more."

Paget waited for the old Scotsman to leave them before turning back to Craven. He looked gravely concerned.

"Is everything truly okay, Sir?" he whispered.

"Better than ever. Now, let us drink!"

He wrapped his arm about Paget and led him to the bar to fill their cups once again. The troops went on partying long into the night in what started several days of heavy drinking for Craven and the Salfords. On the third day Matthys went to find Craven and could not wake him. He was still inebriated from the night before and had not even made it into his bed. He lay sprawled out over the floor of his room, still wearing his uniform. In his frustration Matthys kicked the Captain in the leg. He groaned but did not even rouse. He kicked him in the stomach, and despite a gasp and wince in pain, his eyes opened for a few seconds before falling back into a deep sleep. Matthys felt awful for what he had done, but no less frustrated. He stormed down into the bar below where he found Paget struggling to eat his breakfast. He was not in much better a condition and hunched over his plate in a sorry state.

"Is this what we have become? Drunken layabouts?"

Paget looked embarrassed and ashamed, but he had no answers. It instantly put him off his breakfast, and he sat more upright to present a more dignified impression. Yet there was no hiding his hangover and exhaustion.

"I am going out there to recruit. I can't force any of you to do anything, but I would take a long hard look at what you are doing and ask if it is in the best interests of us all. Soon enough we will go back to the war, and I would have us return strong and with fresh and well-trained soldiers. A few drunken brawlers are not going to win this war."

Matthys turned away and stormed out to go about his work in spite of them.

"Finally, some peace and quiet," Birback groaned. He appeared to have weathered the hangover better than the rest of them but was seemingly the angriest.

The only sober one amongst them was Vicenta, and she sat calmly in the corner of the room watching all the happenings that went on before her.

"How are you so fresh?" Paget asked her in amazement.

"Danger is all around us, and yet you would all drink yourselves stupid?"

Charlie shrugged as she understood the sentiment, she just didn't care. Hawkshaw came down the stairs, but not to join them. He was fully dressed and heading for the door.

"You should not go anywhere alone," insisted Paget.

"I will go, and one of you can take my place when you have sobered up," declared Vicenta.

"Thank you," replied Paget.

Hawkshaw looked to protest but soon refrained from doing so, upon the realisation he would be in good company. They strode out together.

"I have to say, I find it quite amusing to be escorted by a lady, as if the whole world was upside down," smirked Hawkshaw.

Vicenta didn't see the funny side, and that made him feel awkward as if he had insulted her. He didn't know if he should apologise as though he would to a lady or laugh as though he would amongst his fellow soldiers. So, he kept talking to try and move past the whole debacle.

"You know it is quite the peculiar thing, to fight beside a lady."

"Why?" she replied sternly.

"Well, because it is not done. When have you ever seen a woman in the uniform of our army?"

"You chose to join the army, did you not?"

"Why, yes, a most noble pursuit, but I could have walked other paths should I have wanted to."

"Fighting was not a choice for me. The French came to my country and tried to destroy us. I could fight, or I could accept defeat. Could you accept defeat without a fight?"

"Certainly not," he admitted.

"Then you know why I fight."

"The men of your country should have been fighting."

"They did, and it was not enough. Until your country is invaded and taken by force, I do not think you can understand. When was the last time England was invaded and taken?"

"A long time ago, many hundreds of years."

* * *

Craven finally awoke and coughed, causing pain to surge through his body as he folded in half. He dragged himself up onto the bed and lifted his shirt to find the bruising on his body from Matthys' kicks. He had no idea how or where they had come from and shrugged it off as the misadventures of a drunken night. He tucked in his shirt and partially buttoned his jacket before heading to the window. The sun was already going down. He shrugged as if giving up on making anything of the day and staggered down to the bar below to find another beer. Hunt was waiting for him, looking surprisingly cheerful and fresh. Craven took a seat.

"Beer!"

"Oh, no, don't you get comfortable. We have places to be!"

Craven had no concept of what he was talking about.

"Don't you remember the game we have been invited to? We promised to be there this evening."

Craven's face lit up a little as it would be something to occupy his mind.

"We must keep an eye on Captain Hawkshaw, Sir," insisted Paget.

"Okay," shrugged Craven.

"Vicenta said you should take a turn this night."

Craven growled angrily.

"Will you not do it, Sir?"

"The Captain can look after himself. That is what he signed up for."

Craven shot up, eager to follow Hunt's plan and leave behind all of their woes. Paget looked aghast at his unwillingness to help yet said nothing as he watched the two men leave. He looked around for some help and volunteers, but Matthys was still out hard at work, and nobody else seemed bothered. He looked to Ferreira and Gamboa, hoping he would find some joy amongst such honourable men.

"These problems between Englishmen are not our own,

and I would not have it any other way," replied Ferreira, imagining himself in an English prison for having gotten between two officers of the country which they knew so little about.

"Then I shall do it," grumbled Paget.

He would see the job done even if he had to do it himself. He gathered up his things and rushed out to find Captain Hawkshaw, mumbling under his breath angrily as he went. He spent almost an hour asking around at the establishments he knew the Captain had frequented in the previous days until finally spotting him. He was sitting about, chatting with several local men as Amyn watched on from the side, sober and ever watchful, "I will take it from here," declared Paget.

The Mamluk merely nodded in agreement before slipping off into the night.

"Come, Lieutenant, come and join us!" Hawkshaw called to him upon the realisation he was finally in more fun-loving company.

Paget looked uncomfortable and yet felt obliged to take a seat.

"Relax, you are to stay with me, not watch me like a prison warden," laughed Hawkshaw.

Paget relaxed as Hawkshaw gestured for a drink to be brought to the Lieutenant, of which the first sip calmed Paget a little. Although, as he felt the warming beverage go down his throat he instantly felt a little guilt, as though he was consuming alcohol whilst on duty. He would not throw the drink away and risk angering the Captain, but he was determined to go on sipping it slowly so that it might last much of the night. Yet as soon as he had put it down, he found his glass being topped up by Hawkshaw who had a bottle of wine on hand.

Paget slowed his pace as best he could for several hours until finally Hawkshaw was yawning profusely and looked exhausted. He got up to leave, and Paget breathed a sigh of relief. Nothing was more inviting than the thought of his own bed and being relieved of his duties. They stepped outside into the cool and relatively fresh air of the evening, or as fresh as an industrial city could be. Hawkshaw staggered as he tried to keep a straight line whilst they made their way back to their lodgings.

They were halfway there when they turned a bend and found three men awaiting them. They were silhouetted in the lantern light of the streets, but Paget recognised the man in the middle from his arrogant and aggressive posture. It was Timmerman. He could feel his heart almost stop as he looked around for some assistance, but the streets were empty besides the five of them.

"You would attack a drunken man? Do you have no honour!" he cried, trying to find some way to avoid a fight, already knowing it was hopeless. He knew full well the Major had no honour at all and did not even pretend to.

"Leave us," demanded Timmerman.

He had still not shown his face, but vapour arose from his mouth as he spoke out into the cold air. Paget looked around, desperately hoping to see Craven coming to their rescue or any of their friends, but the streets were empty. A shiver ran up his spine as if this was the end, and this was where he was destined to die. The fear was debilitating as he tried to compose himself as best he could.

"Let's get this over with!" Hawkshaw drew his sword and swayed a little to either side, slurring his words.

"Sir, you cannot fight here," pleaded Paget.

"Here and now or somewhere else tomorrow, what matter is it?" he argued.

"You are not yourself, Sir. You must not fight in this condition."

"Must I not? And who are you to tell me what I must do?"

"Someone who cares."

He turned to Timmerman to make his case there, no matter how hopeless it seemed.

"There is no skill nor achievement in defeating a drunken man. Leave us be and fight another day."

"So that you may scurry away to the protection of your friends once more and duck me again?" Timmerman snarled. He drew out his sword, and he and his associates stormed forward with intent.

Paget ripped his sword from its scabbard. He was terrified and yet found some strength to do his duty, but Hawkshaw grabbed his shoulder and pulled him back.

"Do not stand in my way!"

Hawkshaw went right at Timmerman, who attacked alongside his two comrades simultaneously without any care for honour or a fair fight. Paget felt deeply conflicted. He wanted to help, and yet his sense of duty forbade him from going against the Captain's wishes.

He watched in horror and amazement as Hawkshaw engaged with all three men at once. The adrenaline pumping through his body and the danger to his life sobered him a little, and he lashed out at them like a lion, showing remarkable skill despite his state. He beat blades aside in what looked wild swings, and yet still nimbly responded to new attacks to make his parries. He was not nearly as sharp and precise as when at his best, but still would have beaten most men even in this state.

Timmerman was surprised at the struggle he found himself in. But for all of Hawkshaw's defensive qualities, he had no time to respond with his own attacks and was tiring quickly. One of Timmerman's men took a large cloak from his shoulder and waited for just the right moment to cast it out over the Captain's sword. The other two closed in on him before he could retrieve his sword, and Timmerman smashed the ward iron of his sword into the Captain's head.

Hawkshaw dropped to the ground barely conscious with a huge gash reaching from within his hairline almost down to his eyebrow. Blood was already pouring from the wound.

"Get away from him!"

Paget rushed between them, hacking with his sword to put some distance between the three men and Hawkshaw, whose duty it was for him to protect.

Timmerman laughed as he backed away.

"A fiery one, aren't you?"

"We have crossed swords before!"

"Indeed, we have, and we shall again, if you survive this night!"

Paget knew he had no chance against the three men. Even so he was quite willing to fight to protect Hawkshaw no matter what. He was willing to die, and Timmerman could see it, which gave him reason to show some caution. A man willing to die to do what he must was a dangerous one indeed. Loud laughter suddenly echoed out at the far end of the street, and Paget looked back. Nooth and several of the volunteers staggered into view.

"Help!" Paget shouted.

Timmerman tried to press forward, but Paget directed the point of his sword towards his face in the most threatening of ways.

"Help!" he cried out again.

He knew Nooth would be eager for a fight without needing to know who was involved, as was so often the nature of drunken soldiers late at night. The mob of soldiers rushed on towards them, causing Timmerman to scowl furiously.

"Another time!" He strode off angrily into the night.

Paget watched him leave, but only to be sure the danger was gone before he rushed to Hawkshaw, just as Nooth and the others gathered around.

"Captain Hawkshaw, Sir?" Paget gently lifted the Captain up from the cold street.

* * *

A loud crash caused Craven to stir, and he woke up in a groggy state, knocking the cup over before him. Beer spilled out over the table and onto the floor. He had fallen asleep where he sat in the inn he was quartered in. Hunt was asleep on the table beside him, but the ruckus at the door drew his attention as soldiers piled into the room. Paget was supporting Hawkshaw, as a friend would help a drunk back to his bed.

"Too much to drink?" Craven asked in a slurred manner.

"This was not liquor but an attempt on the Captain's life by that bastard Timmerman!" Paget snapped back at him.

Craven was taken aback by Paget's uncharacteristic

language, and he sobered a little upon the realisation that the situation was graver than he gave it credit. He still struggled to contend with the vast quantity of alcohol in his system as was close to incapacitation. He got to his feet just as Paget laid his brother down, and he could see the bloody wound upon his head.

"Who did you say did this?"

"Who do you think?" Paget shouted angrily.

"Get out of the way!"

Matthys stepped in to see to the Captain's wound. He pushed Craven a little, causing him to stumble several paces and crash into a table. He could not find his balance for how drunk he was.

"I didn't do this," protested Craven.

"Yes, you did! You left your post! You should have been there to protect your brother, and all you could think about was the bottle!"

It was the only time the young Lieutenant had ever spoken out publicly against his Captain, a fact not lost on those watching on, as it spoke volumes to the severity of the situation. Paget was shaking with furious anger and entirely unapologetic for his words. He looked ready to throw punches.

"Berkeley!"

A commanding voice roared from across the room. He shot a furious glance towards the sound of the voice only to be suddenly drawn out from his rage.

"Father?"

"What is this? What are you doing amongst these ruffians?"

They looked alike, but his father was six feet tall and well fed. He spoke with an aristocratic accent that was quite out of character with their location.

"I heard my son had come back to England, and yet I did not hear it from you. I had to see for myself, and now I see why you would be ashamed to tell me!"

"I…I…I…" Paget stammered, as he could find no words to explain himself.

"You humiliate yourself, Berkeley, and you humiliate me and my name!"

Charlie had been watching on and desperately wanted to step in and help. Yet she was powerless, knowing it was not a battle she had the weapons to contend with. She had some sense of what a horrifying experience it might be. She had long imagined what it would have been like to raise a child, a privilege that had been so painfully stolen from her years before, and a deep wound she almost never spoke of.

"Do not come home, not until you have your house in order and can act as a gentleman worthy of my name. This war has made a savage of you, and there is no excuse for it!"

"He is more of a man than you can imagine," Craven interrupted with the vague and affectionate ponderings of a drunken fool.

"And you are?"

"Captain James Craven."

"This…this is your commanding officer?" Paget's father gasped, "Then there is no hope for you. I would see to your transfer to anywhere but with this drunken fool."

"Please, no, for you do not know what you do. Under the command of Captain Craven I have achieved great things," pleaded Paget.

"You would follow this pathetic excuse of a man?"

"I would."

"Then go. One of your brothers will rise to be the son I deserve."

It was painful for all to hear. All the Salfords loved the young Lieutenant, and they had all felt they had a hand in raising him to be the fine soldier and man he was today, but nobody dared step in between them. He soon proved he did not need it. Paget's blood was already boiling as his fury with Craven was now fuelled further, and he launched upon his father.

"If only I had a man worthy of being my father," snarled Paget defiantly as he had heard enough.

"You are the disappointment I always feared you would be. I pray you go back to Portugal and never return, for I fear the day you would take my place!"

His father stormed out of the establishment. Charlie was quick to her feet and went to Paget's side, wrapping her arms about him. She felt as much pride as despair for what he had been put through. But within seconds of Paget's father leaving, another tall figure strode in through the doors. It was Mathewson who had his sheathed broadsword in hand ready to deal with the trouble he had heard of. He quickly studied the room and gained a good impression of what had occurred without even being told. Most of all he focused his attention on the drunken Craven, who looked to be in a sorry state and no good to anyone. Even so, the Captain had some idea of his wrongdoing as he found the need to defend himself before any accusations were made.

"Let him handle his own business. That is what you said," he muttered.

But Mathewson was not impressed and slapped Craven hard across the face. It caused him to wake up a little, but he provided no resistance.

"You did not let your brother handle his business. You abandoned your family and your friends!"

Craven had no answer.

"You are not the hero I had read about. You are the very worst parts of the bastard you always were!"

Craven slumped over the table drunk and exhausted, causing Mathewson to sigh in despair. He walked to the door to leave, and yet stopped to address the others one last time.

"Do not put your faith in that man. For he will always disappoint you. Find your own way, but do not tread his path."

He left them in silence, shock, and despair.

CHAPTER 15

Paget paced along, a man at the end of his tether. He looked desperate and in despair, and yet also was looking for something or someone. His uniform was out of sorts but onwards he went as Charlie hurried to keep up.

"Where are you going?"

But he would not reply. She pressed again and again for a response until her patience ran out, and she grabbed hold of the Lieutenant, pinning him to the wall of a shop. Several patrons moved aside but nobody dared get involved in the business of two soldiers who were well armed and in foul moods.

"What are you doing? Where are you going? What are you looking for? Speak to me," she pleaded.

She was close to tears as she could feel her whole world collapsing around her. Her friends were the only thing of value she had, but still Paget said nothing.

"Do not dwell on the words of your father. He knows

nothing of the man you have become. You should not feel shame, but he should."

Paget looked stunned by her revelation, but not for the reasons she imagined.

"I don't care what that old idiot has to say. I care about this family, of Craven and Hawkshaw, and all of us."

Charlie could not believe he could let such biting words fall over him without effect. In fact, she knew for certain they would not. Paget was a gentle soul with so much pride, and yet he had put it all to one side in the interests of others. She was overcome and in awe of his inner strength, but also despaired at the weight he carried on his shoulders.

"How can I help?" She did not want to add to his troubles further and would do anything to lift some of that weight from him.

"All of this, all that has happened to us, and our troubles start and end with Craven. We must save the Captain if we are to save his brother and all of us."

"Save him?"

"He has fallen down a dark path. It is not the first time, and we saved him once before, and we shall do so again."

"You mean the drinking?"

"I mean everything. The Captain has lost his sense of what really matters in this world. The man I followed at Talavera and at Albuera and so many more. I want that man back. The Army and this country needs that man back," he declared as he shrugged her grip away. She did not fight it as she was starting to understand what he was trying to achieve.

"How? How can you change that?" she asked as she pondered what was clearly a very complex question.

"We have to go back to the beginning."

Paget strode on and she hurried on after him.

"The beginning of what?"

Finally, Paget stopped and gestured towards an open door ahead. They could hear the clatter of single sticks and the faint clash of fencing foils as fencers fought past the opening before them.

"Stop running away!" roared a gruff Scottish voice.

Charlie's shoulder sunk.

"You would go to him? After what he said to us?"

"He is our only hope, and I would not give up without a fight, would you?"

She shook her head, knowing she could not say no. They both took a deep breath and went forward. They entered the room to find two-dozen fencers practicing under the supervision of the old Scotsman. He spotted them instantly but deliberately ignored them. But Paget would not back down and made his way around the edge of the room, right up to Mathewson's side.

"Have you come for instruction?" he asked sternly without even turning to face them as he concentrated on his students.

"We need your help," declared Paget.

"Lessons are five days a week and Sunday afternoon. You may also book private sessions."

"We need your help with Captain Craven."

Mathewson sighed and finally turned to face them.

"Why? Why would you keep trying to help a man who would not help you? A man who has given up on his friends?"

"Because I do not give up. I do not let my friends keep

falling. Craven is a deeply flawed man, but there is good in him, and I have seen it so many times. I will not give up, but I need help."

Mathewson groaned as he was coming around, although he was still not convinced.

"We are all forged in fire and brothers bound to the blade. To me that means something, and I think it does to you, too. You helped forge Craven more than any of us, will you abandon him now? Because I will not. I took up the sword to fight, and I will not stop fighting until my work is complete, or I am rendered incapable of doing so. For that is what it means to live by the sword. We do not run from a challenge nor give up when the road ahead is treacherous. I know you did not get this far in life by giving up, and I am begging you now to help us."

Charlie could hardly believe the near poetic words he had woven together. Mathewson could not refuse now, for he had too much pride to do so, just like Paget.

"Then you will help us?"

"Aye, I will, for how could I refuse such a plea? But I must warn you, you may not have given up on Craven, but a man must want to change."

"Yes, but a little help can go a long way."

"You are wise well beyond your years, Lieutenant, and I commend you upon it, for you make a fool of this old man," smiled Mathewson.

"Three years of service in the wars is a better teacher than all my days of schooling," admitted Paget.

* * *

Craven fidgeted in his sleep awkwardly as he dreamt the most awful things. He suddenly felt as though he had been thrown into the ocean as if falling overboard. It was a terrifying nightmare. He hated sailing at the best of times, but his eyes shot open, and he realised he was in his quarters, but soaked in cold water. He shot up to see Mathewson standing over him with a large empty bucket. Craven was stunned as if unsure if he was truly awake, but Mathewson handed the bucket to Paget and exchanged it for a second full one.

"You have let a great evil overcome you, and we will purge it from you as God is my Witness!" Mathewson shouted at him.

He cast the second bucket of near ice-cold water into Craven as he sat up in the already soaking bed. The water crashed over him, and the Captain accepted it was not a nightmare and he was finally awake. He shivered as the water dripped from his body. It was a shock to the system but also remarkably sobering.

"What is the meaning of this?"

"You need help, Craven, and it took this young man to remind me of my duties. For without him you might have been lost to the world."

"Lost?" Craven demanded angrily.

"You abandoned your brother. You abandoned all of your brothers. Hawkshaw was nearly killed last night because you have given up on them, and Paget here nearly went down with him. It is time to get your house in order!"

Craven looked stunned and embarrassed, clearly having no memory of the previous night.

"Hawkshaw? Is he…"

"He will be fine, no thanks to you."

Craven got up with some genuine concern to find his brother.

"Where is he?"

"Did you not hear what I have just said?"

"I heard you. My brother was hurt. Yes, I heard," mumbled Craven.

But Mathewson did not like what he was hearing. He grabbed Craven and slapped him hard across the face. Craven took it and did not know how to respond.

"Now listen to me and listen good!" Craven shrugged but did not argue as the Scotsman went on, "Your brother may have committed some grave sin, but that does not absolve you of yours. This man, Timmerman, who preys on you all, you started that dispute, it was you. You began it all, and you now hide from your responsibilities. These men you command are your brothers, one and all, and you have a responsibility to them. You have forgotten yourself, James."

Craven did not argue. He knew it was true and hated himself for it.

"Craven!" Hunt appeared in the doorway, "Craven, you are missing it!" He stopped in surprise at the scene before him.

"You," declared Mathewson scathingly.

He let go of Craven and turned his attention to the man who had led Craven down a terrible path. Hunt looked terrified and backed away out of the door until his back was against the wall.

"What are you doing?" he demanded in a worrying tone.

Mathewson kept coming. Hunt reached for his sword, but the Scotsman closed even more quickly and placed a firm hand over the pommel, locking the sword in the scabbard.

"I am an officer, damn you!" He recoiled as he tried to resist but Mathewson held him firm.

"I do not care what you think you are, for I know that you are poison, and I will draw you from the wound you have caused."

Hunt tried to resist further, but still he could not release himself from the old man's grip, who appeared twice as strong as him despite his aging years. Mathewson drew out a dirk from his belt, a well-worn and traditional old Scottish long bladed dagger which had become feared with good reason. The huge fifteen-inch-long blade was placed against Hunt's throat, and he could feel the icy steel upon his skin and the razor-sharp edge pressing firmly. He looked terrified, especially when he looked into Mathewson's eyes and saw the look of a man who had killed before. His gaze was colder than the steel in his hand.

"What would you have me do?" Hunt pleaded.

"You are not a man of the Salfords, are you?" Mathewson seethed with anger.

He shook his head.

"Then you will leave and fulfil your duties anywhere else but here, do you understand me?" Mathewson pressed the dagger even harder against the officer's neck.

"Yes, yes."

Mathewson released his grip and pushed him away. Hunt gathered himself up and smiled back at Paget who was watching on.

"It was fun whilst it lasted," exclaimed Hunt before turning and leaving without another word.

"I am afraid we came to England to recruit men. I do not

think we can afford to send one away," declared Paget.

"That man you can. For he does not increase your strength. Far from it, he diminishes it," fumed Mathewson.

Paget felt deeply uncomfortable with the situation, but Mathewson continued before he was able get a word in.

"You asked for my help, and you are getting it. Do not question my methods, for your own have already failed."

Paget fell silent. They needed Mathewson, and he had to submit to his will in return for that help. Mathewson stomped around as though he was completely in charge, and he looked furious. He turned his attention to Craven who had not moved. He was still stunned by the rude awakening.

"Get dressed, now," ordered Mathewson.

Craven looked helpless and did not even argue any further. He knew he had fallen from grace and failed his friends. He submitted to Mathewson without a fight, but most of all he looked to Paget in horror. More than anything he was saddened to see the disappointment in the young Lieutenant's eyes, and the memories of the gut-wrenching experience of the night before was returning to him. He had lost Paget's faith, and it was a heart-breaking thought and a painful reminder of how far he had fallen. He gathered up his things and followed Mathewson with humility.

"What would you have of me?" he asked as they wandered the streets with Paget and Charlie in tow. The others had stayed to protect Hawkshaw.

"I would have you remember the man you were, not the man I once knew, but the man you became in Portugal. I have seen a glimpse into what that man inspired. I have seen your friends fight for you when you had no right to expect it of them.

You inspired men in a way I never believed you could. I always knew you were a great fighter, James, but to become a great leader, that is what impresses me most. Something out there changed you and made you something nobody would have ever thought possible. I want to meet that man, and we are going to find him."

"And if he is gone?"

"Men are what is made of them, and we shall remake you."

"And you think you can do that with fencing?"

Mathewson smiled as he had much more in store for the Captain.

He led them to a field where men exercised and played games, and he recognised many, including Nooth who was stretching.

"What are we doing here?" Craven groaned.

"You see that tree over there?" Mathewson pointed out to a grand old oak standing starkly alone in the middle of the common.

Craven nodded in agreement.

"Nooth has been eager to take another crack at you but let us change the game and have a little fun. The first man to touch that tree and return to me wins."

"A race?" Craven asked in disgust.

"Please, Sir, try this for me," begged Paget.

Craven could not argue, as it was embarrassing enough already to have lost Paget's trust. He felt ashamed and so did as asked, passing his weapons and jacket to the Lieutenant. Nooth beamed with excitement as the two men took up positions. Craven was already sweating merely from the walk to the common whilst Nooth looked fresh and eager. Mathewson drew out his great broadsword and held it aloft.

"When this sword falls, you may begin, and may the best man win."

"Good luck, Sir," insisted Paget with desperate hope and fear in his wavering voice.

The blade fell and the two men set off. Craven remarkably launched from the line as quickly as Nooth, and for the first fifty yards they were neck and neck.

"Come on!" Nooth's friends cried.

But Charlie and Paget were silent as Nooth edged ahead and had a good lead. He reached the tree and quickly touched it. He turned and bolted back towards them, passing Craven with a smile. Craven staggered as he reached the tree and touched it to prop himself up. He coughed violently before throwing up the contents of his stomach. It was an awful sight for Paget to behold, to see his hero embarrassed before the public. He lowered his head in shame and disappointment.

"Do not despair. Not yet," insisted Mathewson as he sheathed his sword.

"How could I not?"

"Many men must reach the very bottom before they may bounce back to what they once were."

"Then this was never a race at all?"

Mathewson smiled at Paget but said nothing as Craven walked back, holding his side where a stitch pained him from the rapid exertion. He looked to be in a terrible way as he made his way back, seemingly ready to quit.

"You knew I could not win, not in this state," he protested at being forced unto an unfair competition.

"But you wanted to, didn't you? To win?" Mathewson

smirked.

Craven nodded in agreement as he had given everything he had to give, and that was clear to all.

Mathewson picked up some boxing gloves from a pile on the ground and tossed them to Craven. The two-ounce gloves offered the slightest of protection to those being struck, but it was a welcome addition to training which many were yet to accept, as all contests and even much training was still conducted bare knuckle. Craven put on the leather gloves stuffed with horsehair. They were supple and well-worn in but also moist from recent use, with an accompanying smell which was revolting, and yet oddly comforting to Craven who had spent so many years as a professional fighter. He gladly accepted the prospect of a fight in favour of the painful run he had just endured. Nooth took up another pair of gloves as the two men moved out into an open area of the field to begin their contest.

"In your own time, begin," declared Mathewson.

"I don't understand. Why make the Captain run a race?" Paget asked.

"To see if he would," replied Charlie.

Mathewson nodded in agreement.

"There is hope yet," added the Scotsman.

"I don't understand."

"I set your man a challenge he could not win, and yet he tried. Craven could have said no and refused. He could have given up. He could have protested before the race had ever begun, but he did not. He gave it everything he had, and that means there is still fight in him," smiled Mathewson.

Paget breathed deeply and sighed. He wasn't so confident and watched nervously as the two pugilists battled it out. Craven was getting beaten badly, although he landed some blows and kept fighting. Blow after blow were exchanged, Nooth exacting his revenge on Craven who did not even have the strength advantage now as he was too weak and exhausted. They battled for more than half an hour when finally, Nooth delivered a massive straight right that sent Craven crashing down onto the grass. He was finished. Mathewson led the others toward the fallen Captain as he struggled back to his feet and peeled off his gloves, nodding in acceptance of Nooth's victory. However, his former adversary did not look overjoyed to have beaten him. It felt like a shallow victory, considering the poor state of the Captain.

"Five laps of the common," ordered Mathewson.

Nooth and the others quickly began the cross country run without protest.

"You, too," Mathewson ordered of Craven.

The Captain struggled to his feet and gasped for air. He looked to Paget once more as if to ask if he could give up now, but Paget would let him. No words were shared, but he knew what he had to do. He took in a mouthful of air and staggered on after the other runners at barely a jogging pace.

"What is it that you are trying to do here?" Paget asked Mathewson.

"Craven thrives in adversity, but he has had none, not since he came home. He has stagnated in an easy existence. For that is why Portugal made such a man of him, isn't it?"

It was hard to argue with the logic, as both Paget and Charlie felt their own lives had been shaped in the same way. They had been forged and tempered into something neither of them could ever have dreamed of, that much was true. Paget watched as Craven struggled on about the large common. At times he managed little more than the weary stagger of an old man in between bursts of a jogging pace that were still far from impressive. Yet on he struggled and passed them with a pained grimace as he attempted to smile. For all of his poor performance, there was a burning fire in his eyes that Paget had not seen since they had left the front line in Portugal.

It was a gruelling day to watch for Paget even though he did not suffer the same struggles as Craven. For hours the Captain went on as Mathewson found new hardships for him to endure. That evening was a very different experience to all the others since their arrival in England. They sat in relative quiet as they ate their supper. Craven looked ready to die where he sat and sipped on water, and yet Birback continued to try and drink the inn dry, belching loudly without showing any shame at all. The room fell completely silent as Hawkshaw joined them. He still wore a thick and bloodied bandage wrapped about his head and remained subdued as he sat down opposite Craven.

"This was not your fault. This was that bastard Timmerman."

"Timmerman is here because of me. He went to Portugal because of me. For any of your sins, I have committed worse," admitted Craven.

Matthys could barely believe his ears as he listened on to Craven laying himself bare before them all.

"He will come for me again," replied Hawkshaw with sadness and regret in his voice, wishing he had never gotten himself into such trouble.

"I will deal with Timmerman," declared Craven boldly.

Paget smiled, as he could see and feel the fire burning

bright in his Captain. Craven was a battered and exhausted man, but in that moment, he spoke as if he carried within him the strength of a hundred men, as though in spite of his condition he could defeat anything and anyone.

"Do not die for me," insisted Hawkshaw.

"I would die for you. For any one of you."

Paget breathed a sigh of relief as he knew Craven had returned to form. He scooped up his cup, held it aloft, and shot up from his chair.

"To Captain Craven!"

For a moment there was silence as they considered all they had been through, but Matthys finally broke the silence and got up to raise his glass.

"To Captain Craven."

The room erupted into cheers as one, united, and of one mind. It almost brought a tear to Paget's eye, but harder days were yet to come. For each day Craven was sober he grew stronger, and Mathewson pressed him harder. On the fourth day of training, he was fighting three opponents at once with his singlestick, and Nooth watched on with glee as he saw the great champion rise to the heights which had earnt him his reputation. Craven's face was battered, bruised, and bloody, and yet his eyes were electrified with energy, and his strength doubled from just a few days earlier.

"What do you think the Captain means by dealing with Timmerman, Sir?" Paget asked Ferreira as they watched from the sidelines.

It was a question which had bothered him for days and yet it had taken him this long to finally ask.

"You know what it means. Craven solves his problems

with the blade."

"Was this not resolved at Portalegre?" Paget thought back to the duel between the treacherous Timmerman and Captain Hawkshaw.

"Does it seem like it was settled to you? Timmerman has followed us all the way from Lisbon. That bastard poisoned the army in my city against us. He tried to burn us alive, and he preys upon us like a starving wolf."

"But they fought, Sir, and under the code of duelling the matter was settled."

"Captain Hawkshaw robbed the Major of another shot, and some would say he did not complete the matter."

"And you believe that?"

"I believe Hawkshaw should have shot him in the heart when he had the chance."

"After so much death, was the Captain not the better man to spare a life?"

"Some lives do not deserve to be spared."

"Then a fight it is?"

"One of them must kill that bastard, and that is the only way this will ever end."

Paget sighed in sadness, as for as awful as Timmerman had been, he was still a fellow soldier who had fought the French beside them all. It was a sad state of affairs that he wanted to see the tail end of, but he smiled at seeing Craven return to form as he took up singlesticks against Nooth once more. Back and forth they clashed, but Craven was both too strong and too quick now as he disarmed Nooth within the first minute. The volunteer bowed in respect at his opponent's victory, causing a cheer to ring out amongst his comrades who had watched and marvelled at the great display of skill and honourable conduct.

"What now, Sir?"

"To battle," smiled Ferreira.

CHAPTER 16

Timmerman laughed allowed as he won a game of cards and collected a horde of coins. He reached for his glass of wine. He partied almost as hard as Craven and yet had no one to restrain him or save him from himself, although the excesses seemed to take far less a toll.

"Another game?"

But his opponents left in disgust, and two of them looked angry and most uncomfortable as if they felt as though they had been cheated.

"You would not like to lose some more?" Timmerman mocked them.

"Not against a man who cheats," muttered one of them.

Timmerman drew out a broad bladed knife and buried the tip into the table before rocketing up to his feet.

"You would call me a cheat? Would you?"

Neither man spoke, terrified at angering him further.

"Not one of you would say it to me, would you?"

"I would!" roared a confident voice.

The whole room was silent as they saw Craven standing in the doorway.

"Well, well, finally you grace me with your presence!"

Craven said nothing.

"But it is with your brother I have issue, or enough issue to demand action," smirked Timmerman, "But you hide your brother like the scared little boy he is, not man enough to come and face me."

Craven said nothing, and yet he was standing tall and bold. Everyone eagerly awaited his response.

"Well? Have you nothing to say for yourself?" Timmerman plucked his knife from the table and waved it about as he played to the crowd.

"Well?" he asked jovially.

Craven finally spoke.

"You fight like a coward, striking at men in the dark of the night when they may not present a challenge."

Several in the room gasped. It was a most grave accusation to make of a fellow officer, as most regarded their honour as paramount above all else. And yet Timmerman was no ordinary nor honourable officer, but he did care about his reputation in a different way. He wanted to be known as a striking and terrifying figure, and not one who scurried about in the night because he was too weak to face a fighting man in a fair contest. Craven knew this and played to the crowd himself and went on before Timmerman could get any words in.

"We both know that after everything this quarrel is really between you and I, and it always has been!"

Timmerman thought on his words but said nothing.

"I will make you a deal, a matter of honour between gentlemen."

Timmerman smiled with curiosity.

"I will fight you. No seconds, no caveats or nonsense, just you and me with swords in hand before all who wish to come and see."

"To what end?"

"If I win, you swear before all present that you will not come after me or my brother again, nor any who serve beside me. All past sins and grievances are to be forgotten!"

"And if I win?"

"You may demand whatever you like, for it is no matter of mine."

"And why is that?"

"Because you cannot win."

Timmerman smirked as the crowd laughed, but the Major could see that the reputation he had worked hard to accrue was now at stake. Craven had walked him right into a trap of which he had only one choice to make, and so he did not have to think about it for long. The crowd eagerly awaited his response and his fearful hold of them was at risk of slipping away from him. Craven had challenged his very character and put it to the test. He nodded along in agreement, accepting what he knew he must or turn away in shame.

"When I win, you will give me your sword. That is all I ask, so that all of England will know that I was the man who bested the great James Craven!"

It would be a great trophy indeed and everyone knew it, for within that sword was all that Craven was.

"I will take from you everything, your sword, your life, and all that your name means," seethed Timmerman.

"Then we shall fight at noon at the ruins of Peveril Castle in two days' time. Let it be known to all far and wide for those who would wish to see with their own eyes. Let there be no doubt who the winner of this contest is. For only conceding defeat or death will end this contest!" Craven shouted clearly for all to witness.

"A fine day it will be," growled Timmerman.

Craven turned and left to a cheer from the crowd, who delighted in the contest which they eagerly awaited. They chatted amongst themselves as they imagined how it might fare, and they let their imaginations run wild. It was a contest they could hardly have dreamed to see. Craven stepped outside to find all his comrades awaiting him, and he stopped in surprise to see that even Hawkshaw was amongst them.

"You should not be here."

"No more hiding, let's end this," replied Hawkshaw.

"Is it done, Sir?" Paget asked.

"It is."

"Then let us be on our way at first light, for it is a long day's ride, and you should be fresh when the time comes," replied Matthys who now spoke as a friend once more.

"Do you believe he will fight fair?" Vicenta asked.

"This is no gentlemanly contest. It will be a war," replied Craven earnestly.

"Then let us retire to the sanctuary we have maintained these past weeks and enjoy the time that we have," declared Matthys.

"Craven!"

The voice had come from a window above them. They looked up to see Timmerman hanging precariously out of it like a madman as all in the street gazed upon him with a mild curiosity.

"Two days, Craven, and I will have your head!"

Craven smiled as those in the street began to talk. Word of the challenge was spreading quickly, just as he hoped it would.

"I'm going to kill you, Craven!" Timmerman screamed at them as they walked away.

"Thank you," declared Hawkshaw as they went on, knowing Craven was risking everything for him.

"No, I should have done this a long time ago. I'm sorry that it took so long."

They reached the inn which had become their home.

"Water!" Craven ordered as he took a seat.

"Not today." Matthys took a bottle of brandy from the barman and a tray of small glasses. He placed them down before Craven.

"You would have me drink?" Craven asked curiously.

"You deserve it. Nobody ever asked you to be a saint, Craven. You do not need to punish yourself forever for your sins. Tonight, we drink." Matthys began to pour and slid one over to Craven, who looked upon it with both desire and suspicion.

"You will never be a sober man, and we do not need it of you."

They all watched on and waited for him, as if expecting him to say some words. He coughed to clear his throat as he looked around at them all, relieved to see the judgement on their faces was long gone.

"Timmerman is a problem I dragged all the way to Portugal and Spain like a cannonball chained to my ankle, forever weighing me down and weighing us all down, and now I have dragged him all the way back to England. If there was ever proof needed to reveal the common factor here was me, then we have it as clear as day. I should have dealt with this problem a long time ago. I cannot go back and change any of that, but I can promise you this. In two days' time, none of you will ever have to suffer his plight ever again. To better days!" He held up his glass in a toast.

"To better days!" they roared.

Craven took a sniff of the brandy, as if to savour the moment, until he saw Birback throw back his glass and reach for the bottle which he drank from directly. Craven smiled before taking a sip as if expecting it might somehow change him, but he sighed in relief as he relaxed back and realised the better days had already come, for they were united and in good spirits. Cheer returned to the room as past animosities faded away and they made merry. Paget stepped up to the bar to get a fresh drink when Ferreira joined him.

"Who knew what four days of hard could do. It is remarkable what the body is capable of," declared Paget.

"Mathewson was not training the Captain's body. Four days do not make a difference to that."

"Then what was the purpose?"

"To train his mind. Craven's strength has never been in doubt, but it is up here where he struggles," replied Ferreira who had far more experience of it, having been there by his side when De Rosas trained them both to break Craven out of his despair in what now felt like a lifetime ago.

"Well, whatever he did, it worked, didn't it?"

Ferreira nodded in agreement as he watched Craven. He sat bolt upright with his shoulders broad and his eyes studying all around like a bird of prey looking out across its territory.

"Believe me, in this condition, nothing could stop him."

Hawkshaw took a deep breath and sighed in relief. The night went quickly as they made merry. Early in the morning he awoke to feel more rested than he had in a long time, for his mind had been at ease despite the impending duel. His faith in Craven was restored, and that faith held firm that Craven would win, no matter what. He gathered his things and went to prepare to depart when at the bottom of the stairs he paused at the sight of Craven, who had awoken even earlier and was enjoying a cup of tea whilst he awaited the others. All of his particulars were gathered and ready, his uniform well dressed and in good order, causing Paget to stop and make a few adjustments of his own to not be outdone.

"Morning Lieutenant," said Craven jovially.

"Morning, Sir," he replied as he took a seat opposite him.

Craven was calm and uncharacteristically distinguished and officer-like, as he moved with precise finesse and with etiquette fit for a Lord's table.

"I was not myself of late, and that is no secret, but I must thank you, for you were there for my brother when I was not."

"As we all are for one another, Sir."

"I promise you I will do better."

"I only ask that you be the Captain I put my trust in."

"I will do my best," replied Craven honestly.

"That is all I ask."

Matthys came down the stairs even more surprised to see

Craven wide awake, having started the day before any of them. He looked impressed but said nothing. It was not long before they took to the road to begin their journey. They drew to a halt as they found Mathewson and several of the volunteers waiting to see them off, including Nooth, who seemed to bear no grudge for his losses to Craven.

"I would say good luck, but luck never won a fight, and you have all that you need already," declared Mathewson.

"Thank you for all you have done."

"It was my duty to ensure you were prepared for battle, and that has not changed. Perhaps it is more important now than ever. For you fight Napoleon, and I would ensure you are the strongest you can be. Valiant defenders of our country, it has been an honour for one who has long combated the perils of a military life to offer the fruits of his labours on the sacred altar of his country."

"You're a good man," replied Craven.

"But you are not," smirked Nooth, which Craven took in his stride with much amusement.

"You would be a great scourge of the French, should you ever want to join the service."

"Still trying to poach my boys, are you?" Mathewson snapped.

"Will you come and see the contest?" Paget asked.

"I am sorry to say that I cannot. I would not attempt to stop you, but I cannot encourage this battle, for I must stand by the standards I set for the men I teach. Duelling is a scourge of our times; may you soon be free of its clutches."

"Then I shall ensure news is sent of the result," replied Craven.

"You need not, for I already know the result," replied Mathewson confidently.

Craven nodded in appreciation.

"Good luck and give the French hell."

"Always."

But for all of his confidence, it was clear there was some worry in his voice. He still looked upon Craven like a son, as he did all who dedicated themselves to the art and science of the sword under his tutelage.

Craven led them on, following paths he knew all too well and needed no maps nor signs. It was not long before they were at the edge of the city and riding out into rural lands. The air was lighter and the smell far sweeter as they all took a good fill of the fresh air, relieved to have left the filthy city behind.

"Why this castle, Peveril, was it?" Paget rode beside Matthys, knowing he would know more about Craven's past life than any of them.

"An old stomping ground for the Captain. A grand old castle built by the Normans, but long since abandoned and left to decay. It is a romantic ruin high up on a peak and commanding grand views across the valley below," replied Matthys as he reminisced from fond memories.

"A ruin, you say? What purpose did it then serve?"

"Any part that we wanted. Mostly it was used for training exercises in the attack and defence of fortifications, both natural and manmade. Peveril Castle reaches high into the sky with steep climbs on all sides and a sheer drop on the Southern face. From the top of that old tower is quite the exceptional view, but not one for those with weak stomachs. No man could survive the plunge from that tower."

"I should much like to see it. I never thought I would get to relive the days of Craven in his Militia days."

"Pray that you do not, for he was wild in those days. A fine fighter he has always been, but his other qualities have left much to be desired."

"But he has come so far since those days, has he not?"

"Yes, but once a rogue, always a rogue."

"And yet you follow him through the best and worst of days?"

"So do you," smiled Matthys.

It was a pleasant ride through the countryside, and as the sun fell low in the sky, they finally spotted it, the great square tower of Peveril rising up into the sunset. It was picturesque. Paget imagined a great may poets and painters must like to frequent the ruins, and yet the only sign of life was the cattle which populated the valley.

The ancient castle was typically Norman, its strong and tall square tower forming it's Keep. A far shorter curtain wall created a large flat courtyard atop the hills upon which the grand old fortification dominated the landscape. They rode up the slopes to make their ascent and were soon riding through the magnificent ruins.

Paget had seen far larger castles in his days, but there was a unique grandness to the ruins, on account of its age and stunning location. The once magnificent castle was reduced to nothing more than a relic of curiosity as it was beyond any defence besides what the land provided it. The curtain walls were low, and much stone had collapsed or been taken. There were no doors nor windows or any wooden structures left which Paget knew must have once been standing. It must have been abandoned for several hundred years. The castle was in a sorry state and yet also beautiful in its fading glory.

Nobody said a word as they made camp and prepared a fire. They all knew what they must do. But Paget had just as soon seen to Augustus and set up his own bed when he noticed Craven was nowhere to be seen, until Matthys pointed towards the tower. He rushed on towards the great tower and found wooden scaffolds leading to stairs into the main gate, which was raised up far from the ground to provide a great defence. The tower was a castle in its own right, as it could have been defended by two hundred soldiers for months or years in centuries past. The wooden boards creaked beneath his feet, and one cracked, causing him to freeze. He looked down in horror at the realisation they were not at all safe. The great stone tower was standing strong and defiant, but the interiors and floors were mostly long gone. The stairways had been patched by amateurs, and he hurried up the wooden steps in the hope they would not collapse as he ascended the tower. He wondered how Craven had managed it, who he imagined was twice his weight.

Finally, he reached the firm stonework of the walls near the top of the tower and gasped a sigh of relief to have a reliable surface under his feet.

"Magnificent, isn't it?"

Paget almost jumped out of his skin, despite expecting to find the Captain at the top. He followed the final stone steps around until he reached the peak, realising it ended with the ragged tops of the walls with no barriers at all. Craven sat atop them, bare to the elements, and with a drop two hundred feet into the base of the tower one side, and far more on the other. At the base of the tower the ground quickly tapered off into a cliff face just as Matthys had told him. Only the great thick walls of the tower itself provided a platform on which to stand. The great height and lack of any safe position to stand made his stomach turn, and so he quickly sat down beside Craven, which at least calmed him slightly.

"We used to come up here to shoot, and to drink."

The thought made Paget's stomach turn further as he could not imagine how his stomach could withstand either, let alone his balance. Craven noticed his fear and discomfort. He smiled and then laughed.

"My dear, Paget, I have seen you face French columns and French cavalry without fear, and yet this is too much for you?"

"It is not natural for a man to stand at such a height, for we would have wings if it were," protested Paget.

"And yet we sail across oceans and do not have gills nor webbed feet."

"No, but at least we float," retorted Paget.

Craven laughed again, and Paget managed to join him. He felt his nerves calm a little until finally they both fell silent.

"This is a fine place for a contest."

"Yes, it is. This place is very dear to me, like a home is to some men."

Craven took in the fresh air as they watched the sun go down. Paget looked deep in concern.

"What is it?"

"The weight of tomorrow strikes me, Sir."

"Do you believe in me?"

"I do, Sir, with all my heart."

"Then you have nothing to fear," reassured Craven.

Paget looked relieved for a moment until he looked out at

the drop in front of them once again, and he became pale.

"Come on, we should get down before the last of the light is gone."

Craven could see Paget desperately needed a way out, for he clearly regretted ascending the tower from the moment he reached its pinnacle, and yet would not back down and admit his fears.

They descended the tower together, and Paget did not seem to breathe until the moment they reached firm ground at the base of the great structure. He gasped with relief and filled his lungs with air once more. It was getting rather cold, and Paget felt the chill more than most, for he was so slight. They could see the fire raging ahead of them. Even so, Amyn lurked in the shadows beside them.

"Go on, warm yourself," declared Craven.

Paget did not need to be told twice and rushed on towards the flames. Craven looked to Amyn and waited for him to say something, but he would not.

"You have something to say?"

"You are at times the very worst man I know, and in other moments, the very best. The fight tomorrow, it is a thing of great honour, the likes of which great poems are written."

Craven was not sure whether to be insulted or honoured by his words, but the fact the Mamluk had come to him at all meant a lot, for he rarely spoke unless he had something important to say.

"This country of yours, England, it is a most curious place. Men who are the best of friends treat one another like gutter rats, and others who profess to be great friends work to stab one another in the back. The latter I understand well, but the former amuses me greatly."

"You have seen the best and the worse my country has to offer, and I would not try to convince you either way, but tell me, what do you really think?"

"To my eyes it is a strange place with strange customs, and yet behind it all, men are still much the same, for better and worse."

"And you, in your country were you the best or the worst of your people?"

"I do not think that is for me to say, but for history to decide."

"Your history is not over, for your people fight on, in the armies of Napoleon mostly, but in you also."

"It will be a great honour to be remembered alongside you," admitted Amyn.

"Even if I go to spill the blood of my countryman tomorrow?"

"Especially for that. For you do not fight that man because you must or because you have been ordered to do so. You fight for honour and for what is right. In my country they would compose great songs about a day such as tomorrow."

Craven nodded in appreciation, but his calm veneer suddenly slipped away as he knew he could speak plainly with Amyn.

"I must do this. I must end this. This feud with Timmerman, he must be stopped. You understand that don't you?"

"That man should have had his throat cut in the night a long time ago, but that would not have been gentlemanly enough for you, would it?"

"Far from it, I don't care about any of that, but I still have my pride, and I would not see a great fighter butchered without a chance to prove myself against him."

"If only the enemy of my people thought like you, for my people would never have been defeated in a matter of honour, but wars are not such a way, are they?"

War?

Craven was eager to get back to it, but he did not look forward to their return to Lisbon, as he was reminded of what a reputation they had gained. Amyn could see the worry and distraction in his face.

"Do not fret about anything but tomorrow, for that is all that matters now. They are all depending on you." Amyn looked to their friends making merry about the fire as if it were just any other day, yet Craven was reminded that they had been through many such nights on the eve of battle before, and this was no different. Better in fact, as he needn't worry about any of his comrades, for only he walked into the line of fire.

"Tomorrow, you walk a line of greatness or death, and I salute you."

Craven took out a small hip flask he had scurried away inside of his jacket and saved until this moment. He opened it and held it up before Amyn.

"Then to greatness," he smiled.

CHAPTER 17

Craven slept easily and deeply, but he awoke to an enormous racket beyond the sheet he had tied to a wall of the castle to make a makeshift lean-to as a tent. He shot up as if expecting trouble but found Paget waiting beyond his shelter.

"What is that noise?"

"Your audience," replied the Lieutenant.

Craven stepped out from his modest shelter to the roar of a crowd as they got their first glimpse of him. More than five hundred spectators had travelled to the castle to see the great spectacle. They had filled out much of the outer bailey and scrambled up onto the dilapidated curtain walls, even to the grand old gatehouse. Some had taken to the wooden scaffolds leading up to the Keep. They cheered at the sight of Craven, and yet his opponent was nowhere to be seen.

"Timmerman has not made himself present, is he scared?" Paget smiled.

But he jested, knowing it was early, and they were all glad to have had a peaceful night to themselves before the clash. Craven did not know what to do with himself. He had several hours to wait, and his clash with Timmerman was all he could think about. He had put it off for so long and now he knew what he must do.

"The crowd are hungry for entertainment, Sir."

"Then give it to them. Some friendly contests with which to whet their appetite."

"Will you join us, Sir? Some light warm up bouts are no bad thing before a contest."

"I may join you," he declared dismissively as there was much on his mind.

Paget did not press further, knowing better than to dig deeper when Craven was focused so resolutely. He looked around for Joze, forgetting for a moment that they had left him in Portugal, for he had long enjoyed the bouts the had shared together. It was a reminder of how much he missed the country, which now felt more home to him than England.

"Wait," ordered Craven.

Paget stopped as he could see a great weight rested on Craven's mind, and it was not the contest with Timmerman.

"What your father said to you is unforgiveable. A man like that may never understand what you have become and all that you have achieved, but do not fret, for it matters not what he thinks."

"Only to my inheritance," smirked Paget.

The thought had not occurred to Craven, but Paget went on before he could find an answer.

"There are more important things in life, though, are there

not?"

"No, not really," smiled Craven.

Paget shrugged.

"I went to Portugal to find my fortune. I do not intend to end this war a poor man, and I would not see you destitute either."

"I am afraid it would take a great fortune to replace what I may now have lost."

"You forget who we face. Napoleon Bonaparte, who resides in a golden palace, living like a king. He took what he has at the point of the sword, and we shall do just the same."

"Honestly, Sir, I'd just be glad to see us all survive this war with our bodies and our minds intact."

Paget walked away, giving Craven a lot to think about.

The Captain understood his sentiment, and he knew that is what he was fighting for this day. Yet he shook his head, knowing the Lieutenant would not be so carefree about wealth if he'd ever had to live without it. He watched as Paget enrolled Charlie, Caffy, Birback, and even Ferreira to take it in turns to fight in friendly contests with singlesticks. It was not the blood sport the people had come to see, but it was enough to sate their appetite. The games went on for some time, and Paget was loving every minute of it.

The audience were clearly growing weary and wanted to see the main event. Paget looked around for some way to keep their interest when he spotted Vicenta on the sidelines. He gestured for her to step into the arena which the audience had created with their bodies. She was glad to oblige as Paget pandered to the crowd.

"Let me introduce you to one of the most terrifying

women in all of Spain!"

The audience booed, for they did not believe it, as if he was tricking them with a circus act.

"You do not believe me?"

"No!" they roared angrily.

"But I have seen it with my own eyes. I have seen her kill more Frenchmen than you can imagine!"

They laughed and jeered. They did not believe him even though he spoke the truth, and yet they seemed to enjoy the pantomime nature of it, nevertheless.

"Birback!" Paget called for the biggest and strongest to face her in what he knew would be just the sort of freakshow fight the baying crowds of the great amphitheatres of Rome would have delighted in. He stepped out of the arena as the two faced one another. Birback knew she was a good fighter, although he did not believe she could win. He was far stronger, and strength had kept him alive thus far against seemingly far more worrying opponents.

"Begin!" Paget ordered.

The audience watched with delight. Not all believed it was a real contest. Even so they watched the entertainment as though it was a scripted play upon the stage. For Paget, he knew it was far from such a thing as he delighted in seeing them clash.

Birback looked every bit the ruffian and cudgel player he had always been. Fast reflexes and a strong body were the tools he relied upon. He barely even formed much of a guard with his body, holding his singlestick out high and with the tip dropping low as so many cudgel players did. Vicenta, on the other hand, moved around him with the grace of a dancer. Birback soon grew impatient as she would not make the first move, and so he rushed forward, snapping a fast cut against her head with the rotation of his wrist. She ducked under the blow and lashed a strike into his rubs, causing him to recoil slightly. He still swung after her in an attempt to do as much damage as he received, but she was long gone before his stick swung by.

The audience clapped and cheered, enjoying the display even if they did not really understand what they were seeing, which made it all the more impressive. She moved with the grace of a fighter who truly knew exactly what her opponent was about to do, even though it was not scripted.

The big Scotsman roared as he charged once again, and yet it wasn't so naïve an attack as he had learnt from his first experience. He attacked just as he had before, setting up his opponent for the same predicted response, of which Vicenta obliged. She thought she was embarrassing him by playing the same trick twice, although Birback turned and braced his stick against his body this time as the blow lashed towards his body. As it struck his stick, he used the energy to rebound into his own blow, hitting her back precisely where he had been struck. She winced from the blow and stepped back to get some distance before nodding in appreciation. She had underestimated the seemingly clumsy oaf.

"He's here!" a voice cried out.

All eyes turned to the old gatehouse as Timmerman rode in with a party of a dozen armed men. He sat high in his saddle, confident and arrogant as if he were a king returning to the seat of his realm. The audience cheered and he delighted in it, but none of Craven's comrades said a word as they watched the devious Major approach as if expecting some last-minute trick. The crowd fell silent as Timmerman leapt from his horse and passed the reins to one of his men. He looked to address the crowd.

"You are here to see blood spilled, are you not?"

They cheered.

"Then enough of these child's games with sticks, let the real game begin!"

Vicenta and Birback were booed out of the makeshift arena as Timmerman stripped off his hat and jacket, and then his shirt. Next was his sword belt, and even from a distance Craven could see it was not the sabre he commonly carried. It was a straight blade, and that piqued his interest.

"Come, Captain, or does fear grip you!" Timmerman played to the crowd as the only man in the arena ready to fight.

Paget looked disgusted at Timmerman treating it all like a joke and with none of the gravity and respect he would expect.

"Are you still sure you want to do this, Sir?"

"Want to, have to, and will," he replied confidently. He then stripped off his jacket and shirt and drew out his sword.

"You have not warmed up, Sir," Paget reminded him.

"I don't need it," he replied, keeping his eyes locked firmly on his opponent.

"Good luck, Sir."

Craven drew out his sword, the only thing which would draw his gaze from Timmerman. He gazed upon the old Andrea Ferrara blade which had seen him through so many battles and what Timmerman would take from him if he lost. And with its loss would go his dignity, his honour, and his very soul. He took a deep breath and looked to Hawkshaw to remember what he was really fighting for. His brother had finally removed the bandages from his head and now bore the long scar running down his forehead for all to see, a mark which would likely stay with him until the end of his days. He could still wear no hat as he waited for the wound to heal and the swelling around it to fully reduce.

"It is not noon, Sir," protested Paget as he tried to find some way to defer the battle even a little.

"What are you waiting for, Craven!"

Timmerman once again played to the crowd, trying to make the Captain look weak.

"The fighters are here. The audience is here. We have all that we need. Let us not wait any longer to be rid of this scourge which follows us everywhere we go," insisted Craven to the young Lieutenant, who looked deeply concerned for him and the risks he was about to take.

But Craven showed no fear, not even a hint of it as he strode forward. The crowd parted and let him through as they clapped with excitement. It was a surreal scene, unlike any duel Paget had ever seen nor read about. The great crowd knew neither man except by reputation and were merely there to enjoy the bloodletting.

Timmerman's associates loomed over the proceedings and were all well-armed. Craven's comrades did just the same. Paget stuffed a pistol into his belt and advanced with his right hand across his body, resting on the grip of his sword ready to draw it at a moment's notice. It was as tense as facing a battle line of French infantry. There was no arbitrator for the fight, no referee nor seconds, or anyone to conduct the proceedings. It was all left to the two fighters who appeared ready and willing to murder one another.

The two men faced off twenty feet apart, giving Craven a

better look at Timmerman's sword. It was remarkably similar to his own, and that could be no coincidence. Craven's ancient blade and well-worn hilt with much gilt rubbed off and a guard which had suffered many hundreds of small scratches. But Timmerman's sword gleamed in the morning light, the hilt of the same regulation form as Craven's but cast in hallmarked silver. The grip was of reeded ivory, and the blade, like Craven's, was neither regulation nor typical. In fact, Craven had never seen another like it. It was almost of a pipe back form, although the reinforcing pipe did not run the length of the spine but offset from the centre of the blade, giving a hollow ground triangular form almost like a smallsword; yet combining it with the cutting ability of a backsword, or single edged cut and thrust blade. The back edge of the blade was sharpened for half its length, a highly unusual feature for the swords of their day. The sword was truly something special and appeared to be brand new. As Timmerman flourished with two cuts in a figure of eight before him, it became clear that the blade was nimble, and yet also rigid and quite capable of delivering a powerful cut despite its speed.

It was a surprise to see Timmerman change his sword and it made Craven smile, for he suspected he knew precisely why the change was made. Timmerman thought he was at a disadvantage and had spent a fortune to try and even the odds.

"What is so amusing?" Timmerman demanded.

"We both know why you bought that blade, but it will be a great gift to my brother when I pry it from your dead hands," replied Craven scornfully.

"Then come and take it!"

The crowd watched silently in awe as they awaited the first clash of blades, having no concept of the tension all around them. The associates of both men watched one another like hawks, ready to see the ruined bailey erupt into a sea of blood at the first moment a move was made by either side.

The two fighters slowly lifted their blades into their guards and approached into distance cautiously until stopping at a lunging pace from one another so that the tips of their blades touched with the gentlest of pressure. It was enough to set up an attack or defence, but not so much as to give away any intentions to their opponent. Craven had forgotten how skilled a fighter Timmerman was, and he looked to be in good fighting shape, and yet that did not bother him at all.

"I should have done this a long time ago," whispered Craven.

"Why wait any longer?" Timmerman spat.

Craven took his advice and erupted into action. He thrust forward and was easily parried away, but he cut around the blade, rotating into a thrust against Timmerman's blade. It pivoted around the parry and plunged his point strongly towards the Major's heart, as if to end his life and the fight in the opening seconds. Timmerman parried it away at the last moment and circled away, laughing maniacally.

"You really meant it. Oh, this is going to be fun," he beamed.

Craven came at him again, attacking with thrust after thrust as though it were a smallsword contest. He disengaged his blade under again and again, probing with feints and interspersing them with full thrusts to land anything he could. Timmerman appeared sharper than ever, especially in light of his nimble blade, which was lighter and quicker than Craven's, although he was able to move Craven's sword away even with the tip of his own in some actions on account of the extra rigidity of his new blade.

Craven could not make any progress, but he was happy to take his time and see what Timmerman had to offer. He gave him a little room and let his opponent come to him. The Major was happy to oblige and came forward with a similar attacking style as Craven as if to mock him, thrusting repeatedly from either side but interspersing them with feints and double feints. It provided no opening in which Craven could safely riposte. After the ninth strike, Timmerman pushed high into Craven's and drove his point home inside Craven's guard but far from his body, as if attempting to stab an imaginary figure standing beside Craven. His plan was only half complete, as Timmerman lashed the back edge of the blade across Craven's face as he recovered.

It was not a heavy blow but a quick drawing one. It opened a shallow but long cut across Craven's left cheek and blood quickly flowed from it. The crowd cheered at the sight of blood as most seemed to have no favourite in the contest, and they were getting just what they wanted. Paget tried to move forward as his grip tightened about his sword, desperately wanting to go to his Captain's aid, but Charlie held him firmly in place.

"Don't, this is not your fight!"

Paget looked frustrated and tried to resist.

"Do you trust Craven?"

He nodded.

"Then respect his wishes," she snarled.

Paget was almost in despair, knowing he was powerless.

Craven had grimaced at the cut when it was first opened, but he now ignored it as if he were some unstoppable machine. He had suffered far worse, and in his gladiatorial days he was quite accustomed to gruelling and bloody affairs. Whilst he was still standing and fighting, the blood flow meant nothing to him.

They crossed swords once more, but this time Craven looked far more determined and focused. He engaged with multiple thrusts just as before and played Timmerman. He responded his quick parries with the tip of his sword, not even bothering to rotate his guard toward the attack, nor direct the forte or base of his blade into the defence as any good instructor would have one do. He was toying with Craven, but the Captain had relied upon that fact and drove his sword forward, just as Timmerman had done to him as if to deliver the same back edge blow. Craven's old Andrea Ferrara was after all sharp down both of its lengths, unlike most swords of the day. Yet even this was merely the second part of Craven's plan, as Timmerman parried with ease. Craven enacted the final step as he took a great leap forward and grabbed hold of the hilt of Timmerman's sword where it lay from his lazy parries. He wrenched the sword down to expose Timmerman's head, slamming the ward iron of his own sword into the Major's head in as close to a mirror of what the treacherous officer had done to his brother.

Timmerman staggered back and barely stayed on his feet. He reached for the wound, wincing as he felt the blood trickle down his hands and then into his left eye. To the crowd it was merely more entertainment, but to those who knew their story it was a hugely personal attack with a great deal of sentiment.

Timmerman looked angry with himself for being so foolish and came back stronger, as both men were done playing games. He hacked at Craven's legs, knowing it would provoke a response high to his own head as Craven's leg slipped out of the way. Timmerman parried this blow with ease as he set up his next strike, but Craven had anticipated it, and they traded cuts back and forth, neither able to find any opening.

Once again, they separated, and Timmerman threw up his sword. He caught it in his left hand and came to guard, expecting to confuse his opponent with the change in angles. Few men ever fought with a sword in their left hand as it was not permitted by soldiers, and it was considered sinister and deplorable by most others. But Craven was not bothered in the slightest. He had spent many years training and fighting against left-handed swordsmen. He parried several blows confidently before exposing the great weakness of a left hander, as after a parry on his right side, he coiled up his hilt high above his head and plunged the point of his sword down over the top of Timmerman's. He buried his point into the Major's shoulder. He cried out and staggered away, trailing his sword before taking it up in his right once again.

There was fear in Timmerman's eyes as he realised what he was up against. He was not facing the Craven of old. A drunken rogue who got by on his old skills, he was now on top form and with a whole new set of skills. Craven would not give him any room to breathe and pressed on with his attack. He nimbly manoeuvred from one side to another, and Timmerman struggled to respond as he moved with supreme skill and timing. He finally entered into a spiralling engagement of Timmerman's sword, giving a quick tap to his hand from underneath. The blow slapped Timmerman's knuckles, causing a knee jerk reaction to open his hand and release his hold on his sword, which fell to the ground. He reached down for it, but Craven grabbed him by the collar and held him upright whilst presenting his sword point to Timmerman's heart, threatening to end him there and then.

Timmerman looked horrified as the prospect of death finally felt real.

The crowd were engrossed by it all, but for the soldiers there to support their fighter it was a tense moment. Craven looked ready to run him through when he looked back to Paget and the sadness in his face. For he did not want to see a man murdered no matter how awful his crimes. He could not help but feel he had failed Paget once and did not want to do so again. He looked to Matthys, knowing he would find counsel without a word needing to be spoken. The expression on his face told Craven everything he needed to know. He could not go through with it. He could not kill the man who had done so much damage. He looked back to his old adversary who was now completely at his mercy. He pressed the point of his sword a little harder into his chest to drive his point home to ensure Timmerman believed he would truly go through with it.

"Yield. Accept defeat before all of these witnesses. Accept that this is over, and that all matters between us and by brother are over, for good," demanded Craven loudly for all to hear without any doubt.

Timmerman only had to think about it for a few seconds to know the offer was better than the alternative, which was death, or at least he believed it was. Craven looked truly ready to run him through. He had managed to keep up the act, which was not hard for him, because he truly wanted to, and was only stopped by his love for his friends.

"Yield!" Craven roared angrily.

"I yield." Timmerman held up both his hands in surrender.

Craven exhaled in relief that it was finally over. He

lowered his blade and the great weight which had rested on his shoulders was removed. But Timmerman seized the opportunity to grab hold of his legs and wrench them out from under him. Craven went crashing down onto the ground, and his sword fell from his grasp. It was thrown well clear as his head bounced from the hard autumn surface. The crowd gasped in surprise and excitement that the show was not over.

Timmerman scurried across the ground to retrieve his sword and rushed back towards Craven. He swung the sword as though it were the executioner's axe, with brutal power and no concern for any return blows. Craven was helpless in the moment as he lay stunned from the blow to his head. He looked up just in time to see the blade coming for him as Timmerman let out a warbling war cry, and yet it was not skull and bone that his blade found, but steel as the blow was stopped just inches from Craven's head. Without looking for the wielder, he knew who it was, for he could see the characteristic pipe backed blade by Prosser which he knew so well, a sword which had once been used to try and take his life and now saved it, the sabre of his brother.

Timmerman backed away a little. Hawkshaw followed with the point of his Prosser sabre directed towards him with murderous intent at the full extension of his arm. The scrape of steel echoed out as soldiers all around them drew blades in readiness for the battle they had been told to expect. Paget's sword was already in hand, and he took out his pistol with his left. Nobody moved in the great standoff as they waited for the other side to do so, or for orders from their respective commanding officers.

"Let us finish this, you and me. No mercy, once and for

all!" Hawkshaw called out as Craven staggered to his feet with the aid of Matthys. He was the only one amongst their party to not have drawn a weapon, and yet they were on his person if need be.

Hawkshaw did not wait for a response. He was going to take his pound of flesh either way. He charged at Timmerman, forcing the Major to defend himself. This new battle was nothing like the finesse of Craven's duel, as Hawkshaw fought brimming with rage. Timmerman backed away as he parried several heavy blows, his light and nimble blade being beaten down by the heavier sabre and determined blows of Hawkshaw who ran him to the edge of the arena. Timmerman retreated through the crowd as they screamed in panic. The blades swung through them, and sparks flew from the steel within inches of their faces.

The armed men on either side looked to one another and could see neither side wanted to fight. They all turned their attention to the brawl between Timmerman and Hawkshaw. Paget stepped up beside Craven as he watched Hawkshaw rush on and attack like a man possessed.

"Should we stop them, Sir?"

"Let men sort it out for themselves," whispered Craven, repeating his old fencing master's advice.

"What?" Paget was amazed at his response.

"No, this is what Mathewson meant. I misunderstood him the first time, and that is my fault, but this is it, this is what must be."

They watched Timmerman try to get in some blows, but Hawkshaw was in fine form and kept up his attack as Timmerman fled towards the protection of the great tower.

They leapt onto the wooden steps and scaffold. One plank gave way under Timmerman who stumbled and fell. Hawkshaw did not give him the courtesy of getting back to his feet and hacked down against the Major whilst he was on his back. Timmerman rolled out of the way, frowning from the pain as he put weight on his wounded shoulder, smearing blood into the woodwork as he staggered back to his feet.

He then rushed up through the doorway into the tower itself. Hawkshaw pursued him relentlessly, cutting and thrusting over and over. Timmerman continued to give ground as he ascended the steps. With one step, Hawkshaw felt his leg fall through. He grasped a rail and kept attacking, as he continued the climb seemingly without any care for his own safety at all. He was focused on one thing.

The audience who had fled in horror now rushed to the tower to get a view of the action once more, but Craven watched from where he was standing. They could hear the clash of steel and occasionally make out both men as they fought past the narrow window slits and ascended the great tower in an almighty clash. Craven seemed to watch on with the same confidence in Hawkshaw as he had in himself before his own fight with Timmerman.

"You are sure he can win, Sir?"

"No, but I am sure we will finally have an end to this madness."

On and on the fight went as the clash of steel echoed out from the roofless tower, amplifying the desperate affair in the most dramatic fashion. Finally, the two men emerged on the walls atop the mighty ruins, the dizzying heights which had so easily turned Paget's stomach. He now felt the same knot in his stomach merely watching Hawkshaw step out onto the same position. Unlike his cautious steps they leapt about with reckless abandon as their blades continue to clash back and forth.

Timmerman was pushed further and further back across the wall as he tried to riposte where he could. He was struggling under the weight and power of the furious blows of Hawkshaw. He was pushed towards a corner of the tower, and he looked over the precarious edge. The fall dropped not only to the base of the fortification but deep into the valley below, the same deadly view Paget had experienced the night before.

With this horrifying sight brought renewed strength and vigour to Timmerman's arm, as he fought back with a will to survive. His blows struck harder, and he ducked under one great swing and turned the tables on his adversary. Hawkshaw now found himself with his back to the sheer drop. It did not scare him as he smiled back at Timmerman in what was one of the most frightening and disheartening experiences of his life. Hawkshaw came forward again and beat Timmerman's blade aside. He hacked against his flank, causing a long cut to open up across his ribs as he staggered back into the same precarious position he had escaped from moments before.

Hawkshaw presented his point towards him just as he did at the beginning of their fight. It was a terrifying signal of intent, but Timmerman felt some loose rocks beneath his feet and looked down. A scattering of mortar had broken apart as the tower decayed. He smiled back at Hawkshaw, thinking he had found the upper hand. He kicked down at the ground, chipping a handful of the mortar fragments into Hawkshaw's face and blinding him for a moment.

Timmerman smirked with joy as he saw his opening. He

launched a powerful lunge from his back foot to send his sword plunging towards Hawkshaw's chest. The pressure he exerted through his back foot loosened a stone for which the old mortar had once bound. The ground beneath him gave way, and he crashed down onto the jagged ruin, his sword falling from his grasp. He began to slide towards the edge and to certain death. He scrambled to find purchase, but the centuries of weathering decay had made the rocks smooth, and there was nothing to stop him from falling. The crowd gasped in horror and excitement as Timmerman slipped over the edge with no hope of a reprieve and felt himself fall freely. As his right hand left the stone walls, it was grasped by a warm sweaty hand.

Timmerman gasped in horror as he looked down at the massive gorge below, realising how close he had come to death. He looked up to see Hawkshaw holding him firmly in place. The Captain reached down, took hold with his other hand, and hauled him up until he was on solid ground once more. They rolled over onto their backs breathing heavily, both glad that it was all over.

"Why? Why after everything would you do that?" Timmerman asked.

"I am done fighting men who wear the same uniform as me. I should have been done with it a long time ago."

"Then it is over?"

"It is," stated Hawkshaw.

Timmerman gasped in relief. He took several deep breaths of fresh air as if he were born again or released from some long time behind bars. His anger towards Hawkshaw faded away. Those on the ground waited with anticipation to see the outcome. Finally, the two men got up together, side by side, and without a weapon in hand.

"I don't believe it," gasped Paget as they watched Timmerman raise Hawkshaw's hand to declare him the winner before all to behold. The crowd went wild as they whistled and clapped and jumped for joy.

"It's over," exhaled Paget, who was more on edge than even the fighters.

"Let's get on with this damn war, shall we?" Craven smiled.

* * *

"Forward march!" cried a volunteer officer, as several hundred men marched from the field of a mock battle to a cheer from the crowd. Powder smoke still wafted by, and Craven and his recruiting party watched on.

"Sir?"

Craven found Nooth standing before him at the salute.

"What is it?"

"If it's not too much trouble, Sir, I would like to sail to Lisbon and fight by your side," he declared. Eight more men stepped up to join him with the same intention.

"I knew you would steal my boys," declared Mathewson as he watched on.

"No apologies. I expect the best, and I know where to find them," declared Craven.

"Not you again?" Paget scowled as he looked beyond the soldiers to see Quicks and three of his friends seemingly at their crime spree once again. The young man strode forward in plain view and right up to Captain Craven.

"I want to fight. I want to be like you." He dropped down on one knee as if to submit to a Lord.

Craven knelt down and lifted him back up.

"Where we are going is hell, but you will be in the best of company. Is that what you want?"

"It is. Mr Mathewson has told me of your exploits. He has told me of what you used to be and all you have become. I want that, too."

"Then come with us to Portugal and Spain and let me show you what the men of Manchester and Salford are made of."

"The French are in for a rough time." Timmerman stepped up to the group with his posse at his back.

Craven looked around for his old Master to make his goodbyes, and yet he was nowhere to be seen.

"Sir." Paget pointed towards the scaffold where he and Nooth had fought a week earlier. Mathewson had taken the stage alone with his sword drawn. He swung it about to draw the attention of the crowd who know hung onto his every word.

"Today these fine men do battle without harm, and they give us a great spectacle, but tomorrow the same men will march to war and to Bonaparte's peril. For there in the crowd is one of our very own. For there stands Captain James Craven and the Salford Rifles, the finest men in the British Army!"

The crowd erupted into cheer as Mathewson leapt from the stage and rushed to the road ahead. The audience began to line it either side to give them a marching out parade. Craven could barely believe what he was seeing.

"Form up!"

Craven and his Salfords assembled with Nooth and his volunteers. Quicks and his pickpockets and Timmerman and his posse were with Craven at the head of the formation.

"Forward march!"

Craven led the ragtag group forward to the roar of the crowd as Mathewson led them on.

"Thank you," said Craven earnestly.

"March with honour, Captain," declared Mathewson. He stepped away and continued to cheer them on.

The crowd clapped and cheered them as they began their journey South and on to Lisbon. On they marched, all divisions put to rest, and with more fighting men than they had arrived with.

"We did it, Sir, didn't we?" Paget asked.
"We did indeed."

THE END

Printed in Great Britain
by Amazon